Wheels Within Wheels

Previously published by Nethergate Writers

Turn Back The Cover (2007)
Roots (2008)
If Stones Could Speak (2009)
Whodunwhat (2010)
A Private View (2011)

Wheels Within Wheels

An anthology of new writing by Nethergate Writers

Introduction by Esther Read

Dundee
2012

First published in Great Britain in 2012 by Nethergate Writers
Website: http://nethergatewriters.webplus.net/
Email: nethergatewriters@googlemail.com

All stories, poems and plays © the contributors, 2012
The right of the contributors to be identified as authors of this work has been asserted in accordance with the Copyright, Designs and Patents Act 1988.

Edited by Esther Read

Cover design by Rikki O'Neill. Website: www.RIKOART.co.uk

ISBN: 978-0-9555831-5-5

A CIP catalogue record for this book is available from the British Library

This is a work of fiction. All of the characters, names, incidents, organisations and dialogue in this collection are either the products of the author's imagination or used fictitiously.

Printed and bound in Great Britain by Antony Rowe & Co. Eastbourne

CONTENTS

Acknowledgements *Stuart Wardrop*   vii
Introduction *Esther Read*   viii

Story Wheel One
Waiting for Spring *Jessma Carter*   1
Thursday *Emma Jones*   5
Felt *Catherine Young*   12
Return of the Corncrake *C.B.Donald*   17
Sgurr Alasdair Traverse *Roderick Manson*   21

Story Wheel Two
Tessie Blunkett's Diary *Beth Blackmore*   29
Mullan *John Mooney*   36
Donkeys and Asses *Derik Hammond*   41
Please Let Me Explain *Jean Langlands*   46
A Clause for Concern *Paul Sykes*   50
Future Sense *Amanda Barclay*   56
Remembering Jay *Elizabeth Taylor*   62
Charity First *Jane O'Neill*   66
Be Careful What You Wish For *June Cadden*   71
The Beautiful Hypothesis *Roddie McKenzie*   76
It Feels Like Years *Chris Smith*   83
Gus'n'Us *David Francis*   89

Story Wheel Three
Trapped *Stuart Wardrop*   99
Family Ties *Fiona Pretswell*   106
Cross *Fiona Duncan*   113
The Cleaner and the Cat *Ann-Marie Aslen*   119

Story Wheel Four
No Hiding Place *Catherine Maidment* 127
Miss Abercrombie's Cat *Helen Taylor* 133
What Elizabeth Bain Did Next *Ann Prescott* 140
Cutting Loose *Mary Davidson* 146
Picky *Deborah Williams-Kurz* 153

Story Wheel Five
The Disc Jockey *Nan Rice* 159
Dial Emma *Ward McGaughrin* 166
Blessings *Jane Stirling* 171
Family Tree *David Carson* 178
Jehosephat *Joyce McKinney* 184

ACKNOWLEDGEMENTS

Books do not write themselves, nor do they produce themselves. Any book is a team effort and none more so than an anthology of poetry and prose like *Wheels Within Wheels*. The various contributions to this, the sixth book from Nethergate Writers, serve as their own testaments to the talent, imagination and skills we associate with writers but tribute must be paid to other members of the team without whose efforts *Wheels Within Wheels* would never have made it onto bookshelves.

Nethergate Writers is the book publishing arm of the 'Continuing as a Writer' courses offered by Continuing Education at the University of Dundee and our sincere thanks are due to Kaye Stevenson and her colleagues for their ongoing support.

The first thing that catches the eye in a new book is its cover. Rikki O'Neill has consistently produced outstanding and much admired cover designs for our productions. This one is no exception – and could be the best one yet.

We are grateful to Ed Thompson for undertaking the arduous but necessary task of proof reading the text, to David Francis for his usual imaginative performance as our Press Officer and to the invaluable contributions made by Jane O'Neill and Faye Stevenson as Secretary and Treasurer respectively.

Finally, we must pay tribute to the imagination and energy of our Class Tutor, Esther Read. She encouraged us to identify and develop the wheels within wheels of the title and to use our skills in producing the stories that lie between the covers. She then changed roles and managed the project from its inception, taking it through the editing process to first draft and from there to final printing and marketing where it ceased to be the 2012 Project and became *Wheels Within Wheels*.

Stuart Wardrop,
Chair, Nethergate Writers

INTRODUCTION

Esther Read

'Wheel: a thing that serves, but only when in motion'
From *The Lacuna*, by Barbara Kingsolver

The thirty writers whose work features in *Wheels Within Wheels* faced a very particular challenge. Given that the nature of any two writers' imaginations, not to mention their writing styles, would be so very different, could they create a story or a poem which would stand alone yet would, at the same time, provide a link to a character in someone else's story or poem?

In the end five different story 'wheels' emerged, some providing a commentary on the often haphazard way in which our lives intertwine, others widening our picture of a particular community or way of life.

Story Wheel One is a good example of both. The stories here are set, for the most part, in the Fife countryside where the pace of life seems conducive to reflection and a strong community spirit prevails. However, this section ends with two very different chance encounters, one in *The Return of the Corncrake*, a story celebrating the restorative powers of nature, and the second in the poem, *Sgurr Alasdair Traverse*, which describes a hillwalking trip to Skye with an unexpected outcome.

Story Wheel Two contains more 'spokes' on the wheel than any other – eleven stories in all. The contrast with the first section couldn't be greater as here we open with a trio of stories exploring the criminal underclass in Dundee before moving to Broughty Ferry where the much more refined character in *Please Let Me Explain* unexpectedly finds herself in a situation with which some of the others might be only too familiar. She links us briefly to London where a corporate lawyer grapples with the cut-throat world of business and a young entrepreneur encounters an unexpected obstacle.

This series continues with a return to Dundee and Broughty Ferry where we are introduced to a delightful pair of Dundee 'wifies' in *Remembering Jay* and *Charity First*. Of course, charity shops attract all sorts. Enter Daphne Le Fèvre in *Be Careful What You Wish For* who, in turn, takes us to the heart of academic life at the University of Dundee. The academic in question shies away from the blind man he passes on the Perth Road who is the subject of our next story. However, it's through the blind man's attempts to sharpen his other senses that we overhear a rather curious conversation between the couple who are the subject of the last story in this series, *Gus'n'Us,* a hilariously improbable romance.

By contrast the mood in Story Wheel Three, set entirely in Dundee, is dark and menacing. We do, however, end in a lighter vein with *The Cleaner and The Cat,* a tale about Agnes, the cleaner of the title, who has unwittingly set in motion the horrific events revealed in *Cross.*

As we move to Story Wheel Four, the community that is the family moves centre stage. We begin with a story of sisterly deception before being transported back and forth in time through the various generations of one family (taking in East Pakistan and India in the 1950s en route) and relocating in Dundee sometime in the 1970s.

In Story Wheel Five the world of local radio, featured in the first two stories, turns out to be rather less relaxed than its friendly image would lead us to believe so you'd think that the services of the hypnotherapist in *Blessings* would be much in demand yet unexpectedly her 'character link' takes us forward into the future in *Family Tree.* From there we make another jump in time to Kenya in the 1970s in *Jehosephat.*

In short, *Wheels Within Wheels* offers readers the variety of styles and genres that they have come to expect from Nethergate Writers. On this occasion, however, there is something extra. As the wheels of one story roll on into the next, we are reminded of the old adage: the whole is greater than the sum of its parts.

Story Wheel One

WAITING FOR SPRING

Jessma Carter

Maisie lived on a farm so she knew about flies, had watched them crawl out from the hay in the corner of the barn and then buzz straight to the door and the light. The first daffodil that pushed its head through limp grass, the first hint of warm wind in your nostrils and the flies came. She had watched them closely, crouched down on her hunkers, near enough to see the red of their eyes, the fine veins in transparent wings, count six legs.

She opened her eyes to the day. Soon she'd stretch to the morning's baleful bleat of lambs, the shuffle of dad's boots across the yard, grandma whisking something in the big brown bowl; no need to pull a sweater over her t-shirt, no need for socks, only trainers as she ran downstairs, counting them, getting to fourteen and straight into the kitchen and the bursting smell of tea and toast and scrambled egg. When the flies came pestering, then so did the bees and the caterpillars and the flouncing butterflies. Maisie was five, ready for breakfast and ready for Spring.

Her father stood at the open door of the kitchen, there as always when she came to breakfast. Dot, the collie, sitting close to his leg, her front feet twitching, ready for more walking. Then her dad came smiling into the kitchen leaving Dot panting and trusting outside.

"We'll go to the school tomorrow, Maisie, if that's alright with you?"

Maisie helped some egg onto her fork with her finger. "I suppose so."

Grandma spooned out eggs for her son and gave Maisie a look. "In my day we didn't get to visit the school before we went. You're lucky, Maisie. You can hae a good look at the classroom and the teacher before you start after summer."

"If I don't like it, do I have to go?"

"We'll discuss that later." Grandma clattered the pan into the sink. "Time was when children weren't consulted."

Maisie's dad gave her a wink and she ate her breakfast, watching the high-stepping hens in the yard, the mist move away from the hilltop, school far away. She ran outside, her grandma's shout, "Watch where you go", trailing her like a worn shoelace.

She had heard them often, the growl of their talk. Grandma, dad, aunt Bella, uncle George, the minister and his smiling wife, the doctor, neighbours and friends, always someone there at night after dad cosied her up. Always uneasy anxious voices, sometimes raised, no laughter like there had been when the heat of the harvest had the men stripped and stretched out in the yard, smiling and pleased as the gold bales bristled pink at dusk.

At night Maisie crept from her bed and looked out of her window. Dad was there again, out of the house, away from the quarrels. She lifted the necklace up to the window and fingered the strange beads made from berries and nuts that the minister's wife had given her. Children had made them and sold them in Africa in order to pay for school. She watched her dad until she grew cold and the beads had dulled. He was looking down towards the road. The fields were brown now, almost black in the fading light except for the one where spikes of pale green winter wheat urged at the earth. He could follow the road, watch it run like a river, dead white under the moon, along to the crossroads where it happened.

From downstairs, words came up to puzzle and tease. It's too much for mother, what with everything else. It's not good for her, here without any other children, all day. It'll be better for you when she's at school. Easier for you. Whiles, you can visit in the daytime. Then the strange words. Prognosis. Coma. A blessed release.

Maisie listened. Just after it had happened, there had been joy, pleasure, tears of relief. She was alive. It hadn't been as bad as they thought. The bones would heal fine; she was a strong young woman. And then it had changed. Talk stopped when Maisie came in the room; a blank silence, not meeting her eyes, stumbling over accidental words, tears not checked.

"Can I go with you, dad, to see her?" And he had taken her. They had driven the bends and twists of the road, turned left at the crossroads where it had happened and Maisie had touched his arm and squeezed it. "See. The road's not cross any more." And he had taken his left hand off the wheel and kept it on her knee while they passed familiar farms. They could see Fred, a small figure down in the dip of the hill, raise his hand to his brow and squint at the sky.

Mum was asleep and very still while Maisie gazed. At home, mum slept untidily. Sometimes her head was huddled under the downie, her long legs sticking out of the bottom, books and specs, face cream, a radio, littered the bedside table. Her head moved on the bed whenever Maisie came in, ready to leap and bounce. Mum would sit up, put her hands over her eyes, sometimes her pillow. "Help help. That can't be Maisie can it?" Then she'd open her eyes. "It can. It is." And they'd both laugh and Maisie would lie in the still warm space that dad had left when he went with Dot on his rounds.

"Mum looks very tidy." Maisie looked at the tucked-in sheet, the water jug, her mum's hands on the cover, the screens. "It's quite like a tent, isn't it?"

Dad nodded. "It's so she won't be disturbed."

"Will she sleep a long time?"

"Quite long."

They watched her breathing. It seemed easy and regular, almost content. "She needs a bit of peace," Maisie quoted her grandma's words. They didn't stay long and kept silent all the way back in the car, checking on one another's thoughts, glancing sideways, one at the other, both uneasy.

School was a long walk for Maisie and although she had chosen to do it she was sorry she had. Maisie constantly pulled at her unfamiliar skirt, ill at ease with her body, her buckled shoes polished and stiff so she had to take care on the farm track. She had passed the school often, heard playground squeals, the bell shouting for order, seen big boys jostle, smaller children swerve, mums waiting and jiggling babies at the gate, locked out from older children who rushed towards them, thrusting bags and papers and hats into their arms, asking and telling. It wasn't like the farm where it was quiet, such noises as there were sifted and lifted in the air tide that moved over the fields.

The seats in the hall were big and hard. Maisie's feet dangled, hit metal legs. A lady spoke while Maisie looked at the other children

WAITING FOR SPRING

squeezed beside their parents. Some of the mothers smiled at her, gave her a wave. One lady brought a big girl to Maisie, took her hand and said that this was Bonnie, she'd show her round and be her buddy.

"Is that your dad?" the girl called Bonnie asked.

Maisie nodded.

"Where's your mum?"

"She's asleep." Bonnie seemed to understand.

"When you've done your work, you can go to the play corner."

Maisie looked at the tables. Scissors, tantalising shiny papers, glue, ribbons, buttons. She wanted to feel the paper, see if it sparkled, try out the scissors.

"What work?"

"Reading and counting and that, of course."

The 'of course' sounded bad. "Is it hard?"

"No, no, dead easy. You'll get it in two winks."

They walked around the classroom. "Try a chair." So Maisie did.

"My mum's a lazy bugger too or so my dad says. Says she sleeps for a battalion." Bonnie laughed loud and long and Maisie joined in to please her.

Walking home, Maisie's hand was curled inside her dad's in case she stumbled on the rough track. "Bonnie says I'll read nae bother. Says I'll learn if I do two winks."

His hand tightened and squeezed hard. "Mum will take me to school when I really start, won't she?" Then it was he who stumbled. "She'll wake when all the flies come and the butterflies. I told Bonnie my mum wasn't a lazy bugger, she was waiting for Spring." Maisie looked up at him. "She is, isn't she, dad? She's waiting for Spring."

Maisie ran to the door where Grandma stood, looking beyond Maisie to her son, a boy still, with an old man's pain. She held back from touching him and asked, "Did she take to the school?"

He nodded. "She'll be fine."

THURSDAY

Emma Jones

It was obvious that the day was mauve before Fred stepped outside. He surprised himself, as the day was Thursday. Thursdays were generally purple. Fred felt, though, that mauve was close enough to purple not to let it matter too much.

The toast had gone cold in the wire rack, just how he liked it. Exactly half an inch of hard butter lay waiting on the plate, yellow. Spreading it evenly over a triangle of chewy bread he concentrated on reaching the edges. Looking at the clock above the Aga he checked in. 6.14 am. No need to rush. He sat back, biting out a semi-circle of perfection. The teapot was still warm and the tea stewed, as usual. He poured the dark liquid into the striped mug and set the pot back, cosy in its red wool.

Fred's home-made welly warmers sat snugly in his boots by the door. Heated wine bottles fitted easily into wellington boots. In January welly warmers were essential. The copper kettle whistled, ready to fill the pipe-defrosting irrigation tube. It ran directly from the back door to the frozen water pipes around the yard. Fred hated defrosting pipes; the hot water scalded his numb, plum-coloured hands. Satisfyingly, this invention almost always worked. Buttoning his overalls to the top he looked out of the window. The sky, Stilton blue vein, reminded him to pack his cheese sandwiches.

Twenty-seven years had started in the same way. Fred had taken a holiday only once but the bedroom had been beige and there was no butter at breakfast.

Rather than waste time, Fred would think. Often, after he thought, he would formulate something to make his life easier. Life on the farm wasn't necessarily simple, even after all this time. Outside now, the yard was treacherous; concrete holes, like jelly moulds, collected clouded rainwater. Overnight it froze, levelling to create a lethal shell. When the winter sun awoke, the yard looked like the

THURSDAY

surface of the moon. The holes should have been filled in during the summer when the days were long and orange but Mr Wallace claimed it was too expensive. Fred noticed he had started to leave his car up the lane, rather than navigating the yard. Fred tried filling the holes with gravel, which lasted about six weeks before it needed to be done again. He would have to give it some more thought.

Mr Wallace owned three farms in the area. Fred had worked for worse people. The tractor, once green, started first time in a choke of grey. Fred could drive to the far field with his eyes closed; sometimes he did. He enjoyed using his invisible-gate-opening-mechanism made from plastic water bottles and fishing wire, especially in the cold weather. It meant he could stay in the relative warmth of the cab.

The field was solid mud tarmac, his tyres barely denting the earth. Jobs were fewer this time of year, but took twice as long. Fred worried. He hoped he would not be replaced like the rusting gates or the sagging fences. Mr Wallace had finally agreed that Fred should renew them all, during this winter. Since he started this, Fred would end each day a rich amber, stained deep into his worn skin.

The project for that day was gate number four; he slowed on the approach and as he rounded the hedge it came into view. He braked sharply. It was pink. He turned his head to look over his shoulder and then back again. Gate number four was pink, not rust brown. Hot pink. He stopped. Pink. He jumped from the cab, forgetting his joint-saving bungee hand-cord. His knees flashed red as they took impact. Fred looked right, then left. He reached out and touched the smooth gloss. It was cool and shiny and dry. He ran his hand along its length. He held on tightly as his mind chased his thoughts; it fogged black and he wobbled. Closing his eyes he breathed deeply, one breath, then two. In then out. The pink line scarred the inside of his eyelids. Eyes open or closed, he could not get away from it. He perched seriously on the footplate, which was wet. He put his head to one side and considered his predicament. He realised he had never seen a live flamingo. He wondered if the day was still mauve. The fog cleared, a little. It was Thursday after all.

The best thing about Thursday was Mrs Wallace. Mrs Wallace wore mustard-yellow hairy gloves and visited once a week, on Thursday. Fred looked forward to the tasty goodies she left under the checkered tea towel on the kitchen table. Today, however, he knew he needed to talk with her. There were at least three and a half hours before she would arrive. Removing his tool kit from the cab he worked hard for two hours, methodically loosening pink nuts and bolts. He clipped three karabiners along the top of the gate at exact intervals and flipped a light switch on the side of the trailer. The gate lifted up slowly and as it swung neatly across, he used a computer joystick to guide it into place. He smiled, satisfied, as it worked perfectly. He climbed up in the back of the trailer, swapped over the clips to the new gate and then reached for his flask. Lukewarm tea transferred the pink outside, inside.

Fred saw the pristine white estate travel the first half-mile of the lane from his perch in the cab. It crossed the railway line moving towards him and then disappeared behind brittle tree silhouettes. Fred started the tractor. The engine chug blocked out the low rumble from the car. He knew he would get to the house first.

The kitchen was cosy but Fred paced the cold larder from where he could get the best view of the lane. The car bonnet winked its arrival in the passing sun. Mr Wallace climbed out of the driver seat with difficulty; the gloves he wore were green. He coughed, glancing around; he rubbed his arms, cold. Cherry streaks of broken veins stained his cheeks. He started to move towards the house.

Fred watched, waiting for the other door to open. He couldn't see the mustard gloves. He froze, feet stuck to the floor. She hadn't come. He started to panic but Mr Wallace approached the passenger door. Relieved, Fred moved to the kitchen. He sat waiting, fingers warming, occupied with scratchy twine inside a working pocket. Green gloves entered first carrying the tray covered with a checkered tea towel. Fred fretted. That wasn't how the tray came in; something was wrong. He dared not look up. The twine caught again and again against his rough skin.

"Aw right there, Fred?"

Mr Wallace was talking but Fred couldn't understand. He could see the mouth moving but could hear only sounds. Two teeth were brown.

"You OK, Fred? Look like ye've seen a ghost."

Mr Wallace was still talking, looking at Fred and pointing to the checkered tea towel on the table. Fred closed his eyes, breathed in then out and opened them again. Mr Wallace had sat opposite him. Fred's naked hands pushed together like a pyramid.

THURSDAY

"Mmmmrs Wallace?" Fred tried his own mouth.

"Aye, that's right, Mrs Wallace. So that's settled then Fred. I kent ye'd understand. Enjoy the quiche... and we'll keep this oor little secret, eh?"

He left. Fred lifted up the corner of the tea towel. Red and green poked out from glazed egg flan. He heard the car start, reverse then move steadily out of earshot. He sat. The copper kettle whistled. He took it off the heat and left the kitchen. Outside, in the back of the trailer, gate four was still pink. He thought. He worried. He wondered what his and Mr Wallace's secret was. At 3.15pm he realised he had not eaten his sandwiches. He reached into the back of the cab and into the brown paper bag.

The sky was Scotland-blue by 4.52pm and outdoor work had to cease. Even though Fred had wasted most of the day in confusion, his job tally was as it should be. Heading indoors he thought he saw a light in the far field. He peered out. Nothing. It must have been headlights from the road. He prised away his wellies and slid off his overalls. Often he would mend sacks or socks in the time before tea. Tonight he felt like doing neither. For a while he stood by the window staring out, willing his eyes to see further into the dark. Night-seeing spectacles, now there was an idea. He thought long about the fact that potatoes have eyes. Then he saw a light again, scorching through the shadows. Certain this time, he dressed quickly, grabbing a torch from the cupboard. Outside he could make out his breath, white. He hesitated; the tractor would be quicker but noisy. He looked at his feet. Pity his rollerskate adapters only worked on concrete. He proceeded by foot, slowly. The air was syrupy. After about ten minutes he got to where he thought the light must have been. He turned his torch off.

"Hello? Who's there?"

He listened. There was no reply. He tried again.

"Hello? I saw your light from the house. I know you're hiding."

Nothing.

He switched his torch back on, the beam, like a hedge cutter, slicing through the gloom. Nothing was out of place though a faded orange cigarette butt caught his eye. He stood in silence. Five minutes later he walked back to the house without using the torch. He started to train his eyes for night vision.

Inside was carrot-orange cosy. He realised he had been foolish to leave quickly without gloves or a hat. They lay abandoned on the sideboard. He was hungry, having forgotten about dinner. His tea was now late. He set cutlery, one place mat, poured a glass of water and buttered a piece of bread. Reaching in to the cupboard he removed a white plate with a blue rim and excitedly folded back the tea towel. He could not believe what he found. He looked around the kitchen but there was no one to blame but himself. The quiche had gone cold. It was hardly surprising. He looked up at the clock it was nearly seven. Tea was always at half-past five.

He discovered the red was tomato and the green, broccoli, and even though it was cold he had an extra slice and a second piece of bread. He thought as he chewed and concentrated on the conversation he had taken part in earlier. Words flashed up as he attempted to piece them together.

Surprise

Handbag

He hadn't heard of a surprise handbag before and felt a little sad he hadn't thought of it himself. He imagined a clasp opening and a bright green snake shooting out. He remembered there was a cucumber in the fridge.

Was it party or painting? He couldn't fathom it.

Secret

Quiche

He knew the quiche wasn't a secret as he had eaten it. He rubbed his brow.

Niece

Field

Fred tried a thinking technique he'd discovered himself. He would imagine himself in an empty white room. Hopefully the words he was searching for would come bouncing in through the door like on a children's television show.

Church

Then a word bounced in that made him drop his fork and it crashed loudly onto his nearly empty plate.

Kill

He remembered Mr Wallace's scarlet mouth open, laughing. It was now eight o'clock. He knew he had to act, but he wasn't sure how. He looked at the phone. He dared not use it unless it was an emergency.

THURSDAY

Was this an emergency? He wasn't sure.

He tried to take his mind off it by filling the sink and started feeding the dirty dishes through washing brushes made from bottle cleaners. Generally his plates sparkled. He wondered if Mr Wallace really had told him that he had killed Mrs Wallace, after she had cooked a quiche in a field and the niece was coming to go to the church. He looked at the phone again. It was cream. Mrs Wallace had written the number in blue biro on the pad years ago. It was still on top. He lit a candle, he enjoyed the golden glow. It flickered, he turned off the big light.

His fingers shook as he tried the number. The dial ticked slowly back into position. He counted, seven rings before the click. It was noisy.

"Hello, Queens Farm?"

He swallowed. He thought it was her but he couldn't be sure. It was loud. He heard Mr Wallace in the background, laughing. His mind flashed one word. He dropped the phone. It dangled on its twisted cord, swinging above the floor twice, three times. He grabbed it and slammed it down, making it ting in anger. He sat down at the table and enjoyed the silence.

He jumped when the phone started to ring. The sound filled the whole room. He ran to it but paused before picking it up.

"Hello?"

He answered cautiously, quietly.

"Hello Fred, everything alright there?"

It was her, it was Mrs Wallace. He thought of ham and mustard sandwiches.

"Aye, fine Mrs Wallace." He pressed the receiver hard to his ear.

"Right, well that's good. You phoned, you see. We called 1471. You don't normally call that's all, so I just thought I'd check to see if everything is alright. I thought perhaps you might be ringing me to say happy birthday?"

"No, I don't think so."

"Oh."

Silence.

"Right then Fred, see you on Thursday. Hope you enjoyed the quiche?"

"Aye."

"Right then, bye for now."

"Bye."

He kept the phone to his ear, hoping for more.

"Oh, Fred, are you still there?"

Fred breathed out.

"Aye."

"Mr Wallace told you about my niece Sheila, didn't he? I hope she didn't make too much mess with the pink paint. She's such a tearaway and we thought it would keep her busy for the afternoon. We knew you would replace the gate soon enough anyway."

"OK."

"Right, bye then."

"Bye."

He replaced the receiver. He was happy Mrs Wallace was still alive. Actually he was sure everything was fine. The day had been purple after all.

FELT

Catherine Young

"Where's thon jumper o' mine?" her husband asked.

"I've not mended it yet. It's needing a…"

"Oh, here it is, I'll just put it on." He pulled the grey woollen over his head and plunged his hand through a large hole in the elbow.

"I was just trying to tell you it's needing a patch knitted. That hole's rattled down too far for darning."

"It's been on that mending pile of yours for ages. Seen the day you would've knitted a new jumper in the time."

She sighed. "Look give it here. I'll do it this afternoon."

He took the jumper off and tried to fold it before putting it back on the pile.

"It's just it's braw and warm for the lambing."

"I know. It was good wool."

She re-folded the pullover. It was both the colour and texture of porridge. It had been lovely to knit up.

She'd need to have a good rake through the scraps box to find what remained of the original wool. Her husband was right, though. Once upon a time she could have easily knitted a whole new jumper in the time she'd been putting off mending this one. She'd lost interest in her knitting somehow.

It had always been an afternoon job for the sitting room, when all the tough kitchen chores of the morning were done. The radio would be on in the background. It was her quiet time to herself but still her hands would be busy with knitting for the family.

In the afternoons she could stop worrying about pinching and saving and where they would get the money for fixing the whatever it was that needed fixing that week. There was always something in the creaky farmhouse that needed doing. A quick fix. A make do and mend. A never quite done once and done right, only *until the next time*. So problems were never solved, just emergencies staved off for a while.

Catherine Young

Her life wasn't as she'd imagined. It wasn't a challenge any more. She could rise to a challenge. She was strong. She was resolute. She was inventive, creative. But this was relentless. It'd stopped being fun a long time ago.

She'd learned the rhythm of her day from her mother who'd learned it from her mother who'd done it in a big house for somebody else. She did the must dos, the boring, the tough hard jobs first. In the morning. Or perhaps it was the *someone else would notice* jobs? She was never entirely sure. Maybe it was the jobs that could be measured. Full laundry basket, empty laundry basket. Doing the laundry first thing was obviously a logical choice in her mother and grandmother's day but for her, in the days of washing machines and tumble driers, the timing was purely psychological. It was so she could see she'd made some progress. And it *could be seen* that she'd made some progress. Anyway, if the chores were out of the way she felt she had earned a little time to herself. She was allowed. Allowed to stop and think, except she never did just quite that nowadays.

How long could she put off and put off? Forever? Could she keep dodging it till that big loud voice became a whisper? Too tired itself to keep on going, if always ignored. But things didn't work like that.

It was the ball of turquoise blue wool in the scraps box that had brought it all back this time. She remembered knitting it that really bad winter. She'd liked the cheery colour and since the wool was four ply rather than the double knit she always used for her husband, she'd had fun trying out a few fancy bits around the edges. That had been a big mistake, what with the colour *and* the fancy stitches it had been deemed a *girls' jumper* and her son refused to wear it. Even his friend, the quiet lad who liked bird-watching, had turned up his nose at it.

It was only moss stitch but that frivolous effort of pattern had caused too much bother, so she sat assiduously unpicking the over-sewn seams then unravelling the kinked wool in a loop from her hand to elbow. The moss stitch edges had been almost impossible to pull down, the wool often knotting, and needed her sharp metal unpicker to slice through a stitch only for her to start all over again. These strands of yarn were small fragments sometimes only a few inches long. They were no use for knitting but she kept them in squiggly lines draped over the small table next to her. Maybe they'd do for something. Once she got on to the stocking stitch section it fairly rattled down, yards at

FELT

a time. The jumper shrank away before her eyes with barely a hitch. Within minutes the whole back of the jumper was gone. Hours of knitting disappearing as if the effort had never taken place. The only evidence in fact was in the regular kinks in the wool; unending peaks and troughs.

To make the wool reusable she tied the skeins off and carefully hand washed them in the kitchen sink. That was a morning task for a good day, as it required the half moons of wrung out wool to be draped over the washing line to drip dry. It took all day and was never quite done, the wool ending up by the fire in the evening to air off like a damp dog.

Next, the dry skeins of wool had to be wound around her hand one way then another to make a round tight ball. Ideally, each end of the skein was over someone's hands, arms apart and thumbs erect, arms gently swaying as the end of wool was pulled back and forth to be wound up. An extra pair of hands made light work of the task but it was an unpopular chore what with it being an evening job and requiring some attention. If need be she could make do with the back of a chair but then *she* had to do the swaying as she wound the yarn into a ball; a rather tricky and cumbersome struggle on her own. After all her efforts the wool was never straight but the kinks loosened enough to make re-knitting possible though never easy.

She re-used the turquoise with a navy she'd unpicked from a school jumper and hoped that the two blue stripes would be judged suitably boyish. She was doing garter stitch – all plain – and making it fairly baggy so it could be worn for a while. This kind of self-sufficient reusing materials was what she'd often daydreamed about years ago. The romantic notion of Ma, Laura and Mary in their *Little House on the Prairie* creating beautiful patchwork quilts over the long winter from remnants of dresses, each patch recalling a flashback to a happy time when the item had been worn. A party perhaps for Mary, or a bit of a scrape for Laura that would always end up all right in the end. Pa and Ma would see to that. Art maybe imitated Laura Ingles' real life but there was not much in her own life that she would want to re-imagine.

This small square grey garter stitch patch for her husband's sleeve was turning out to be one of the most difficult things she'd ever knitted. Every few minutes she'd look up and gaze out the kitchen window. The girl who rented Gamekeeper's Cottage was up at the sheep field and was a welcome distraction.

The girl and her boyfriend had been to art school and called themselves artists when they came to look at the place but the boyfriend's work reference for the rental agreement said he worked full time as a barman and she knew the girl helped out waitressing at the hotel at weekends. They seemed nice enough though and were willing to put up with basic facilities in return for their smallish rent.

Her husband didn't grasp the fact that people paid ridiculous sums of money for a bit of luxury and as for holiday lets... Farm diversification was a dirty word. Maybe in an ideal world farming should be about the land and the beasts, but they didn't live in an ideal world. The pair of them were getting older: they worked hard and for what? The farms were looking more and more rundown. Getting him to go over the books with her, even once a month, was becoming impossible. There was always a ewe needing looked at or a fence come down.

The artist girl was often up at the sheep field. Every few days she'd see the scarlet dyed hair – that matched their old car – bobbing about at the fence. At first she thought it might be for brambles but it was far too late for them now. She was intrigued. It was hardly the best view on the farm if she wanted to draw, unless maybe she was drawing the Suffolks. She always thought they looked a bit like old wifies with white perms. But the girl was only there for five or ten minutes at a time, then the red car would scoot down the lane again.

It was half an hour later when she'd finally finished the patching that there was a knock at the door. The artist girl was wearing an Arran jumper, jeans, muddy brown leather boots and a bright red and purple waistcoat with a flower pattern up the front.

"Hi, it's my car, Mrs Wallace. I was wondering if I could get a tow from a tractor. It's just that I'm running a class in an hour and I really need the work," the girl grinned, "what with the rent due next week."

She laughed at her cheek. "Here," she said, grabbing her keys from the hook by the door. "I'll give it a go with the Land Rover. I just love that waistcoat."

That evening her husband wandered in to the sitting room carrying a mug of tea.

"What's that you're doing?" he asked.

"It's felting. That artist girl from Gamekeeper's Cottage does

FELT

workshops in the village hall. I gave her a lift earlier when her car got stuck. She dyes the wool off the barbed wire fence."

"Right," he nodded. "Is that soap you're rubbing into it?"

"Mmm. You build up layers of wool and work it till it kind of melds together. It's quite therapeutic."

She lifted a layer of netting off the top. "Thought I'd make a cushion. What do you think?"

"Aye. It's braw."

She took a deep breath. 'Those wee squiggles of turquoise are off that jumper I had to rip down. Remember, because it was *too girly*. And then when I'd re-done it, he never got the chance to wear it." There, she'd said it out loud. She didn't dare look up at him.

He paused. "Don't remember the jumper but I mind the arguments right enough." He touched the damp felt. "He was a right stroppy wee git, even as a young lad." His finger traced the blue line. "But he had a good way with the beasts. Would've made a fine farmer."

He placed his hand on hers for a moment. "Thanks for mending this." He picked up his jumper, put it on and went back out to the lambing shed.

RETURN OF THE CORNCRAKE

C.B. Donald

I'd been there for half an hour and had made a decent list already: tufted ducks, various finches and tits, goldeneye, goosander, mute swans, robins, dunnocks, a treecreeper, a heron, the pheasants, siskin, two great spotted woodpeckers and of course the ubiquitous mallards. Still no sign of any grebes though, but it was early in the day. A perfect early March morning. Almost no wind and that crisp feeling only spring dawns can bring. Best of all, the crannog hide to myself. My brother had decided to go hillwalking and I hadn't protested. I poured a refill for my coffee and rejoiced in the perfect silence, broken only by the calls and hoots of my feathered companions.

I'd only just finished congratulating myself on my fortune when I heard the dreaded sound of footsteps coming to my hide. Drat.

I did my level best to affect a lack of interest in the newcomer as the door opened, preferring instead to gaze at a distant blob through my Nikons. Was it a gadwall? I hadn't seen any of those for ages. It could just be a mallard. This called for the scope, at my right hand side. As I reached over for it, I saw him for the first time.

At this hour in the morning and out of the tourist season I'd fully expected another birder like myself. He didn't look like any birder I'd ever met. Tall and needle thin, his most notable feature was a large tattooed spider's web on the side of the neck facing me. He was dressed in a crumpled tracksuit and Burberry ensemble complete with baseball cap. He had an into-the-wood haircut. And no sign of binoculars. A shiver ran through me. Though he was seemingly intent on staring out of the right window – the opposite one from my vantage point – into the tall reeds, I still felt very unnerved knowing there were probably only the two of us within miles.

As he turned to talk I saw that he had sunken cheeks and eyes that looked like they hadn't seen sleep for days. I hoped he hadn't registered my shock or worry. He nodded a little to me and seemed to think he had to say something to break the silence. His harsh guttural and slightly slurring voice was entirely in keeping with his appearance.

"Lovely mornin', innit?"

I mumbled some sort of agreement. Though it had been benign, the greeting didn't make him any less intimidating. Here I was in isolation with someone who clearly had no business being here. Why had he come? As he had turned to look out of the window once more I snatched glances at him with the eye that wasn't fixed upon my scope (though in any case I had lost sight of my potential gadwall and wasn't looking at the loch at all now), trying to sound out his intent and looking for any menace. I couldn't see the bulges of any weapons at least, although he'd surely be expert in concealing them. I had my own knife but it was in my rucksack some five feet to my right, and no closer to me than it was to him. If he did suddenly lunge my way I'd have no chance of getting to it.

I noted that he was fidgety, shaking even. My stomach churned. What did the spider web signify again? Was it that he'd killed someone in prison (or was that the teardrop)? He let loose an ugly and violent snort then looked in my direction again.

"Sorry, mate. Ah'm rattlin' the day."

What did that mean? Should I be reassured or even more alarmed at his rattling?

"Hope ye dinnae mind if ah talk tae ye a bit. It helps, ye know?"

"No, it's fine," I lied, as convincingly as I could. I spotted his left leg was tapping rapidly and repeatedly on the hide floor.

"Ah've no' been in wan o these places fir years, man." His hand was going to one of his pockets. I tensed. He produced roll-up papers and a tobacco tin. "Ah'll jist roll wan up fir later." I nodded, nervously. He was probably in his mid-thirties, although with his mouthful of broken teeth and flesh taut on his bony frame he was in such wretched condition that he could have been a fair bit younger. I could not concentrate at all. It was in danger of spoiling my bird count, this visit of his.

"Ah used to come tae bird hides wi mah granda." I could hear a choke in his voice as that sentence trailed off. "Well, ah say 'come' but it was mair like ah was dragged, kickin' and screamin. Ah hated every fuckin' minute. Wanted tae be oot wi' mah mates. But..." His story was interrupted by another horrible snorting noise before he resumed.

"The auld man fair loved his birds. He was ayeways tryin' tae get me interested, but ah was never up fir it."

I was silent. I just didn't know what to say to him. I was listening anyway: it wasn't as if I had much choice in the matter.

"He used tae talk aboot his favourite birds as being 'corncrakes'. Ye know whit they are, chief?"

I nodded agreement. I'd seen some of them on the Western Isles in the past. Unprepossessing little things, but each to their own. "Yes, I've seen them before." I was a little less nervous now he was at least talking about birds, even if he clearly knew little or nothing about them. At least he was making an effort.

"Really? So he wisnae jist makin' them up then?" A little chortle followed. "Stupit soondin' name for a bird, that. He used tae drag me aroon' lookin' for them. Said he used tae see them a' the time when he was growin' up but he hadnae seen any fir years. Ah dinnae think he saw any again." He trailed off and began another scan of the loch from his window, clearly deep in thought.

He wasn't so bad really. Pig ignorant, certainly, but there was a warmth in his tone about his granddad that reassured me. Not much chance of him seeing a corncrake today though. They'd been long absent from the lowlands and, indeed, most of the mainland as farming methods had killed them off in all but the fringes of the West and the isles. It was too early in the season for them too, being summer visitors. I heard him stifle something that could have been a sob. I tried to engage him in conversation, not wanting him to get emotional for whatever reason. Best to exercise his intellect.

"Er... how did you end up here then?"

"Ah goat the bus frae Perth and then legged the rest. Nice day fir it, anyway." Another short pause while he looked around, perhaps having seen something in the long reeds. Something was moving over there right enough.

"Ah thocht tae mahsel', well... this could be mah last chance tae come tae a place like this fir a good while. A fuckin' long while." He gave a laugh which contained no mirth. Gallows humour, I suspected. I gulped a little, suddenly reminded that this guy was probably as hard a case as the schemes produced.

As he talked I could see something coming out of the reeds: a great crested grebe swimming away into the loch with some purpose. I

RETURN OF THE CORNCRAKE

suspected he was getting ready to display. Sure enough, he turned and began to swim in the opposite direction, from where he had just come. I could see his partner emerge from the reeds and swim towards him. The ned and I were in for a treat.

"Haw, man," he exclaimed, "whit are those birds up tae then?" He was pointing at the grebes. Not even he could have missed them.

"It's a mating ritual," I replied. "They'll display to each other and the male will maybe even present reeds to his mate to help build their nest. Look."

He was looking, all right. I even lent him my binoculars at that point (though had to help him use them), as I already had my scope pointed over there. The grebes swum until they were face to face and begun their dance, an elegant and elaborate mirror image of each other with heads bobbing up and down, back and forth and up to each other, almost appearing to kiss. I'd seen it all before, but through his eyes got a ravishing new insight into it, almost like it was my first time seeing it too.

We watched for a good while, soundless, as they went through their whole ritual for our eyes. I heard him quietly sobbing again, and, much against my expectations and better judgement, I could feel my eyes fill with tears too.

By the time the birds had moved back into the rushes we had both composed ourselves and normality had resumed. He turned to me, eyes rheumy.

"That wis magic, mate. Thanks." He gave me my binoculars back, surprisingly tenderly. "Granda kent whit he wis on aboot efter a'."

He got up and made to leave. It seemed like he'd done what he had come to do. As he got to the door he turned back to me. "Whit birds were thae yins by the way?"

"Oh… those were your corncrakes, mate."

He left with a wide smile cracking across his crooked mouth.

SGURR ALASDAIR TRAVERSE

Roderick Manson

1) South-West-Ridge from Bealach Sgumain

The Mauvais Pas,
illicit offspring
of an Alpine Chimney
and a bad Bad Step
who mated on a thunder day,
gives way to a dead-scales staircase,
a Bloody Stone dark
in the shrouding mists,
whimpering of vertical
if we could see the drop.

But the steps are good
and many
and the options varied
for the feet
and hands
and the fact
we cannot see the way to go
a detail
among many we ignore.

We go
til there is no more up
to go.

SGURR ALASDAIR TRAVERSE

2) Sgurr Alasdair – Summit

Even on this smallest peak,
anorexic
with a basalt gut
unravelling in the east,
there is the urge
to build
a cairn.
We add a stone –
the social obligation,
some might say.

Around,
there is the cloud below
and all along the ridge
the teeth
of long dead dragons
tear the sky
in shards of bloody blue
above the fire-flayed grey.

Roderick Manson

3) Sgurr Thearlaich

Above the Chanter of the Stones,
where the south-west piper
howls,
a wall of rock.

An old, good rule –
when you cannot go up,
go round –
and sure enough
the wall relents
to give us access
to the saw-bright edge
of a prehistoric tooth
in this gabbro-basalt jaw.

It grinds the sky;
we smile.

SGURR ALASDAIR TRAVERSE

4) The Great Stone Shoot

A thousand feet
of glacier
in stark, dismembered rock
edging north
in imperceptible decay
until a swimmer
breasts
its waves.

We are
by no means
synchronised
but down we go
surfing the plaque
of long decaying teeth
in this dead
but vicious
jaw

until the ridge fights back
and a rock
of fist size
flies above the waves
as if a bird in flight
but with intent.

Roderick Manson

5) The Rocks Remain

My last bad step
is upward
as that bird becomes
an intermittent flock
of malice.

I climb until I see the three -
why did I know it would be three? –
who laugh with gravity
and without aim
until they see their images
are captured
on my phone
and I tell them
where these images will go
when we get down.

Three is too many
and I,
the one,
should go.

The measure
of the mountaineer
is not to climb
but to survive.

Story Wheel Two

TESSIE BLUNKETT'S DIARY

Beth Blackmore

Extract from the diary of a fourteen year old girl.

This Diary belongs to Tessie Blunkett.

SATURDAY - Morning Headline

Tessie Blunkett has moved house. Again! (Read all about it).

Tenth time Ms Blunkett has moved already! Which school she goes to isn't her problem. Who'd have her? She has an a..tti..tude problem. Says it's perfectly alright for a fourteen year-old lassie. Who has strictly got her own opinions. Which she gives free-of-charge. Cos she don't care a bugger what people think of her. Especially Charlene Handy and her ugly gang of chavs. Who think they're great. Think they're dead popular. Tessie says she wouldn't join them, even if they all said **pl..ee..se.**!

Mam's pushed a blue face round my bedroom door. Covered in a facial. What a sight for sore eyes. Mam's shouting. In highfalutin' language. *If yoo go oot, Tessie, yoo have to gie the secret knock to get back in!* That's cos it might be the polis, or the man from the social that keeps knocking our door. I'm away to try a facial. Cos, guess what! I will be fifteen on Monday! Yahoo! Pressies! See ya.

1.02pm - Headlines

Good news –	Tessie Blunkett's cheeks are feathery soft.
Good & Bad news –	Rain's pelting hard seagull-shit off the windows of the Blunkett's mucky new high-rise flat.
Worst news –	Tessie's chin is like pepperoni'd with bright orange plooks!

TESSIE BLUNKETT'S DIARY

Yesterday, Tessie and her string-pink-hair Mam, and Mam's here-the-day-gone-the-morrow toy-boy Scarpo (nothing between his ears 'cept hayfever, a dangling fag, and a homemade black-eye) scarpered out of their stinking flat. With a heap of new clothes (price tags still on and all!) stuffed in co-op bags. Now they're holed up and hiding in another shitty pad. Tessie says her voice echoes out from all the bare places. New address definitely not supplied.

Yesterday Mam bagged her anti-depressants, vodka and coke, heated-rollers, straighteners, facials, umpteen 'Heat' mags. Scarpo bagged his fags and cans and one girlie mag. (Mam gave it the OK). I bagged my dodgy laptop, CDs and personals. Asshole Scarpo bashed my laptop off the stair-wall. Now it takes longer than Mam's hangovers to boot up! Geez. Mam's yelling like an auld fish-wife. Tessie! Where's ma bloody pills, hen? Someday the cops are going to bring them, personally!

8.09pm - Tessie Blunkett Meets an Angel!

Ms Blunkett says the rain began peeing down when the three of them vamoosed across the bridge in the dead of last night. Then they had to squelch up hundreds of stairs (lift scuppered) to this horrible flat belonging to a friend of a friend of Mr. Scarpo's – Gabriel Mullan. Mr Scarpo calls him Angel. Tessie's Mam calls him more like a criminal, a bastairt, an a crack addict. Tessie Blunkett smells beans-on-burnt-toast. See ya.

11.11pm - Tessie Blunkett is Lady GaGa's No. 1 Fan!

Tessie Blunkett watches Lady GaGa on anything. She sneak-reads books, mags, newspapers. In shops. When nobody's looking. She says Lady GaGa is fab…yoo…lus.

Oh my God, I love her. She's amazing. She had on a man's top hat with a veil. For an interview! She says she's a passion-holic. So am I! She says her whole life is theatre. That's like acting, eh? My God, turns out she's only a bit older than me. And, was bullied at school! I'd even eat a raw tomato to meet her. 'Baby I was born this way…oolala'. And swap stories… *oolala*. Scarpo says I've a great voice. Could be in her backing group… *oolala*. Says I should dress like her. Turns men on. Dirty bugger. Mibbe I could invite her to my birthday party.

Beth Blackmore

Dear Stefani. (Honestly, that's how you spell her name).
    My name is Theresa Angelina Blunkett. You probably don't know it, but we've got the same middle name. I'm your hugest fan. I can hardly believe you left home so young. Got the cheapest place to live in. And ate shit until somebody would listen. I'm definitely going to do that. How did you manage to walk in sixteen inch heels? Do you get on well with your sister Natalie? I'm so like you Stefani, I like boys a lot too. Would you believe it? I was born on March 28 **same as you.** *Mibbe we could spend the day thegither if you like. Congratulations on selling all those albums and singles. Lots of love, T.A.B.*

Geez. I've come over all embarrassed. Mam and Scarpo just gone out for fags. To settle their nerves. Mibbe a good draw will settle their punches. Hey! Its *food* I need. I'm starving – need protein. WAIT! Something's scuffling. Right outside our front door. I need a knife.
    I'm OK. Does a werewolf have a barking laugh? Honest to God, I thought a werewolf was prowling on the stairs. I smelled something big-n-hairy. Like, definitely something in the dark bits was holding its breath. Turned out to be a man wearing a fur-coat and five-inch heels. One of them gripped in a hairy fist! Face painted like a clown. Said he was looking for Kitten Caboodle. Told him to try a pet shop. Said I could come to Kitten's party if I put the knife down. Told him thanks, but no thanks, cos I had an appointment. I'm cutting a solo single. Geez.
    What if I was completely alone in the world? Might be safer. What would I do first? Eezee. I'd find the best pad in town! Get me a long pink limo. Go find Lady Gaga's sixteen inch heels. I need to wear them! Like, step into her shoes. Become famous for being famous. You asking how I become famous if I'm the only one in the world? How could I *not* be famous! Hah! Who's going to stop me? Think about it. And I'd never need to *ask* for a birthday present ever again. Please no! Sounds like a shindig's starting outside our door. Sounds like junkies dancing up the walls again. Mam calls them the neighbourhood watch. Mam! Where the hell are you?

1am – Somebody tried to kick-in our door. Freaked out. Kept schtum. Crawled way down inside my duvet cover. Got stuck. Nearly suffocated. Why do I have to put up with shit like this? I'll tell you as it is. It's cos life's not like some nice baby book, that's why! Like…

TESSIE BLUNKETT'S DIARY

> Once-upon-a-time, Tessie Blunkett was born. Beautiful.
> Brought up good by nice parents.
> Got a medal for attending school.
> Chooses Uni.
> Becomes a Psychologist.
> Marries a Prince.

Fat chance. Mind you, I'd like to learn to read people's faces as well as books. Safer. Anyways, I live in the real world. More like…

> Once-upon-a-time, Tessie Blunkett was born. Ugly.
> Started by some nowhere dad. Plenty of Uncs.
> With ogley eyes.
> And odd toyboys. With hard-ons.

Beginning and end of my pathetic life-story. Make it up or leave it. I do both.

2.31 am - You know how I'm a kinda all-over-the-place person? Well it's made me psychic. Like, I feel vampire cockroaches are crawling over my scalp. And I can see mirages of the Gorbals. My pals there! I was in Hell's Angels for lassies. I'm going to write something in case I go back to my old school. See Mrs Beattie again. She liked my kind of writing. *You're good at description, Tessie. Just watch your language.*

Dear Mrs Beattie,

Advert - Pad for Rent - In Vampire City
Windowless bedroom pad. Ideal for vampire lovers. Tight squeeze. No canines. Closing the door is like shutting the lid on a coffin. Dong! No baths! Why not stake it out. Fires a no-no. Choose from our Rare Garlic-Free Meat Burgers. Bury yourself alive in lavender-scented black-silk sheets. Holy Crow! Batty twilight shenanigans included. Definitely a place to die for.

Hope you like it, Mrs B. Thanks-a-billion for the 'Twilight' book. I fancied Edward Cullen. When he **wasn't** thirsty! I think bits of me are very like Bella and bits are not. I'm kind of clumsy, definitely stubborn, sometimes a terrible liar. (You could always tell. Cos I bit my nails.

And chewed chunks of skin off my bottom lip. Sorry. Still do it. Still get sore ulcers that nip like billio when I eat stuff). Serves me right. Mind you, Edward had a pile of bad habits. Like, he couldn't keep his fangs to himself. Hah. Hope to see you soon. Love from Tessie B. xx ps I'm nearly fifteen. Can't wait!

Nearly 3 o'clock. Nearly too tired to write. Eyes clapped out. Torch clapping out. Can only see to write one word at a time. Sentences growing short. Scarpo never screws the nut. Barged into my room. Definitely a nono. Not up for his screw-loose stories. Hold on. Got to sling him out on his ear!

Same old shit. *Honest, Tessie. You're a dead ringer for Beyonce.* (As if!) *Tessie, hen, I know a guy who'll give you singing lessons.* Hah. Last dead-brain eejit sucked on a moothie! Sent Scarpo to look for double AA batteries. He better find some or I'm definitely going to report him to Mam for barging in.

Arrgh! Shadows have arms, legs, fingers. Long necks. Creeping Jehoshephat!

I've got Mam's gold-cross necklace on. If I can't get to sleep, I'm going to get Mam. Ever feel you're running out of time to get anywhere? Geez. Fifteen on Monday! I bet Mam's got me the coat hanging in 'Oli Chic's' window. It's awesome! Short, all black pattery material. Has thick lace all the way round the bottom and a huge shiny belt round the middle. Costs £149.99! Definitely fit for her princess, Mam says, so she's going to get me it. For sure. I'm going to take a dander down the street tomorrow to check it's gone out of the window.

Listen to Mam and Scarpo giving each other laldy. The talk in the Blunkett jungle is that we're to move like, real soon. Mam says it's time for a parting of the bloody waves. Think she means 'ways', cos she doesn't believe in Moses. And she was glowering right through Scarpo. Can you part ways with yourself? I think Lady Gaga did that. Please God, let me get her 'Judas' CD for my birthday. I've asked for it a hundred times.

Sunday - Afternoon Headline
Tessie Blunkett finds a New Pal - This is a true story!

Tessie met Celestina Vanska when she went out for curry sauce on chips and a dander down the road to go look at her new coat. What a lovely name. Celestina.

TESSIE BLUNKETT'S DIARY

It curls up inside your tongue. Celestina was fighting another lassie that ran away screaming. Celestina asked Tessie for a fag and then vomited all over the pavement. Only Tessie Blunkett helped her. What a nice girl she is. Celestina she means.

It was too horrible for stupid words. Celestina and that bitch were bawling obsen...itics at each other. Celestina ripped a big handful of hair out of the ugly bitch's scalp as she was legging it. Then it got better. A right laugh. A man with a long brown face and hundreds of big black freckles cruised past three times smiling at us. Even though Celestina was as white as a sheet she waved back. She said he was always on crack. And if we waited long enough, his smile would still be there hours later. Definitely had the same smile on his ugly mug after three roundabouts on the road. Then he pulled down a window and whispered out loud to Celestina. He could hardly get the words off his big pink tongue. Cos he kept sucking his big wet lips in and out. But I definitely heard it. Hey Tina, how's about a wee piece of ass?

    Tina had silly clothes on. All her bare bits had red and white patches pinched thegither with the cold. She hung inside his car's window. Probably he was trying to get Celestina to get me to join them. Bloody hell. His huge hand kept rubbing up and down her arm. And it was missing a finger! Celestina's promised she's definitely going to try to come to my party tomorrow. Fingers crossed. Ha!

5.36 pm Told Scarpo I met a Mafia man. Didn't listen. Too busy sticking a whole bunch of birthday stickers all over his bare legs and chest. Like. Fat chicks make me horny. You're sexy, sweet n' sassy. Girls kick ass. He asked me a joke. *D'you know why lassies are called birds?* I started putting on a boiled egg to take to Celestina. *Tessie, think aboot it! It's cos of all the worms they pick up. Get it, hen? Yoose lassies would eat worms tae get a man.* Told you. There's nothing between his ears.

    Anyways, to finish my story about Celestina. She said I'd better go or I'd get picked up by the polis, or worse. By a punter! I know that word. Don't go there! Poor Tina has very long daddy-long-legs. I didn't think anybody in the world could have it worse than me. I felt better when I got back in our flat. Door locked. Then remembered I forgot to check out the coat. Can't wait for tomorrow!

Beth Blackmore

Monday! Happy Birthday Tessie! - Fat chance!

Nearly 2 pm. Birthday over. Mam and me were huddled thegither listening to Scarpo crying buckets outside the door. Mam inside spitting feathers. Actually at the start of my party the three of us were having a good time. My Barbie cake had a candle that exploded into a firework. With the window all blacked over, it was awesome. We had Pepsi and everything. And laughing and feeling about in the dark for pressies. Played statues. Scarpo was stoned! Spoiling everything by bumping into me. Mam couldn't leave her inhaler lying around or he'd have puffed himself to death. Then he got maudlin remembering his pal Andy the Superman. Who fell and broke his skull wide-open climbing out some window to look for a fire escape that was never there in the first place. Next thing Scarpo gets more ridiculous. He keeps falling down dead-like on the floor every time the people upstairs stopped playing Alice Cooper's *Welcome 2 My Nightmare*. Next thing, he and Mam had a fisticuff argument. She called him a retard. He fell out the front door in a giant huff. And Mam wouldn't let him back in. Fed-up writing about it. Bye.

Best birthday present ever! Bestest! Bestest! Bestest!

Just heard! Mam's friend Sheila is taking us in! That means I can take my letter to Mrs Beattie myself. Cos Sheila lives beside my old school. '*Baby I was born this way… oo… la… la*'. And I can practice on Sheila's high heels! Bad news is, I don't have enough nails left to nip out the wee glass bits buried into my new coat. Worst news of all, there's no time to tell Celestina we're moonlighting. Hang on! Somebody's knocking on our door. Knocking makes a change! See ya.

MULLAN

John Mooney

Mullan headed for the Tally Ho bar, its boarded up windows blending perfectly with the barricaded shops on either side. He was quite familiar with an early morning need for an alcohol fix but this was a new experience: six waking hours without a drink. No wonder he was thinking about chasing his first pint with another.

"Big Issue, mate," cried a vendor outside the bar.

"Fuck off," Mullan rasped, without raising his head. He pushed the swing doors of the Tally open and walked in amid a friendly hubbub, which diminished slightly but noticeably as the doors swung behind him. He nodded silently to a group playing dominoes before reaching the bar counter. The barman started to fill a pint without comment before Mullan climbed on the barstool.

"Danny about?" he asked, swallowing a throatful of dry phlegm whilst watching the amber nectar push up the frothy collar to the top of the glass. He followed the froth's slow progress with a throat that ached.

"Danny?" the barman replied without taking his eye off the beer tap. "Danny's dead."

Mullan looked at the barman for some sign of misdirected humour. "What tae fuck dae ye mean?"

"Danny topped himself. Have you no heard or have ye been an overnight guest of Her Majesty again?" The barman then placed the now full pint tumbler on the bar counter and without releasing his grip on the glass, announced, "£2.35."

"When? How, for Christ sake?"

"Nae idea, that's all I know. £2.35."

Mullan counted the money from out of his pocket, then considered more questions but caught sight of an old man sitting next to the open fire reading a paper. He took his pint and walked over to where the man was sitting, pulled back a chair and sat down. No word of greeting came from either of them.

"What's this aboot Danny?"

The old man looked up over the top of his paper with only his eyes visible. "Aye, he topped heesel apparently, but apart frae that, I know nothing. I'm meeting Bomber later, he'll know."

Mullan made no comment but sat turning his glass through his fingers. "Tell Bomber tae gie me a bell, will ye?."

"Aye, OK, Mullan."

"How did *you* find out?"

"One of the lads in the domino team there has a cousin in the polis. He told him this morning."

Mullan stood up and drained his glass. He glanced over at the domino players, hesitated, then left the pub, its friendly hubbub seeming to rise again as the doors swung behind him. The *Big Issue* seller, watching him pull up the collar of his jacket and head into the wind towards the city centre, raised two fingers behind his back.

Topped himself? Stupid bastard, Mullan thought, then a sudden realization caused a smile to form itself around his three-day growth of beard. He was thinking about the £150 quid that Danny had loaned him. Good timing if nothing else, he thought. The smile was replaced with a frown as he stopped suddenly, put his hand in his jacket pocket and after rummaging among cigarette papers and matches, produced a door key. He moved through the narrow streets sidestepping burst bags of discarded rubbish without actually being aware of where he was. Suddenly he stopped walking and looked down at the key. Danny had some good gear in that flat of his. Could be worth checking out before anybody else got there. After a pause he turned right and walked with more purpose and with a quickened step across open waste ground towards some high rise flats.

An hour later in Danny's flat, Mullan had three bin-bags in the middle of the floor. He had stuffed £35 and some loose change he had found in a drawer in his pocket and was shifting the rest of his loot into the three bags. Booze, DVDs, ready-made meals, tins of beef, in fact anything that could be useful or sellable went in. He twisted the necks of the bags, tied two together and slung them over his shoulder like two saddle-bags. He was just giving the place the once-over in case he had missed anything when he noticed a mobile phone and an envelope lying under a coffee table. He pocketed the phone and opened the envelope. Inside were five copies of the same photograph showing a man in dark glasses driving a car and beside him a young woman, looking as if she was caught unawares by the camera.

Not exactly Danny's type. Certainly not regulars in the Tally.

He turned the first photograph over and written in an almost illegible scrawl were the words, 'Stephanie Lomond Thursday night'. Underneath that was a mobile number but it was the next line that hit him between the eyes. '£400' had been crossed out six or seven times and replaced with '£4000'. Mullan pocketed the photographs alongside Danny's mobile, hitched up his 'saddle-bags', grabbed the third one by the neck then left, leaving the door of the flat wide open.

Now back in his own place, Mullan sat in front of a large TV screen paying no heed to the excited chatter of the commentator as a race at Kempten Park was reaching its climax. With a can of beer in his right hand he awkwardly manipulated the buttons of Danny's mobile with his left until he could see the array of text messages. Thumbing through the list he stopped at one whose sender number ended in 6000. The can was discarded whilst he searched his jacket pocket. Producing the envelope containing the photographs he checked the mobile number on the back of the first photograph. It was the same. He opened the text messages. Once he had read the contents of the message, Mullan drained the can.

"Well, Danny boy, what the fuck have you been up tae? What have you got on her that's worth four grand?"

Two more cans were emptied. "And why five copies?" He checked the text messages again but none ended in 6000.

Perhaps if he had only drank half as much beer, he would have come up with some more important questions but for each of the ones he did ask himself, he always came up with the same answer, four thousand.

He picked up Danny's mobile, hesitated, then pressed a few buttons.

"Hello". The voice was posh. "Hello?" it repeated, then irritably, "Who's there?" Mullan sat in silence until the line went dead.

He pulled another ring off a can and read the text message again. His fingers massaged his hairy throat, then hovered over the dial button. He hesitated, moved his fingers to scratch his chin then put the mobile down. From out of his pocket he retrieved a tin of tobacco and some cigarette papers and began to roll a cigarette between his smoke-stained fingers. Once alight, the cigarette was positioned into the corner of his mouth leaving enough room for the contents of the can to be poured in. He took more time than usual to finish the beer but when the last few drops dripped onto his tongue, he pressed 'dial'.

"Hello?" The same voice was a little cautious now.

"Stephanie?" Mullan asked.

"Who is this?"

"I've got the photograph." Mullan listened to the five-second silence, then belched.

"Who are you?"

"Friend, friend of Danny."

"What do you want?"

"Slow down doll. Let's talk." Mullan relaxed a little.

"About what?"

"The picture, doll, let's talk about the bonny picture."

"I think you have the wrong number." There was a click then silence.

"Bitch." Mullan re-lit his dormant cigarette and leaned back with his head on the back of the couch. He had some thinking to do.

Half an hour later, a ringing phone woke him from his thinking. It was Danny's.

"Aye, What the fuck is it?"

"What do you want for it?" the same posh voice asked.

"Oh," Mullan was awake now, "it's you. Changed yer mind then?"

"How much?" The voice was sharp, dry and businesslike.

"Well, let's see... what about... eh..." Numbers flashed through his mind. Then his train of thought was interrupted.

"Four thousand. Bring the photographs with you tonight at eleven o'clock. All of them. We'll be at the railway bridge on Magdalen Green. Be alone."

"We?"

There was a pause, then, "Yes, I'll be walking my dog." The phone clicked into silence.

Mullan sat for a few seconds then stood up, one arm in the air.

MULLAN

"Re... fucking... sult! How about that then? Four grand, ya bastard."He celebrated by opening another beer. Then celebrated more.

The thumping overture of the Ten O'Clock News roused Mullan. He switched the TV noise off. A dry throat and fuzzy head caused him to search for relief but every one of the vessels that might have brought respite were lying askew on the table and floor, squashed, leaky, and empty. As the local news followed silently, he was barely aware of the screen images before him. He took no notice as a policeman in a fluorescent jacket was being interviewed with trains passing in the background.

At 10.40 he closed his front door with a bang that would have woken the neighbours, had he any. As he made his wavering way up the street, heading towards Magdalen Green, he was unaware that his telephone back in the flat was about to ring. It rang eight times before the caller was asked to leave a message.

"Hey Mullan, it's Bomber. You've heard then. He did it last night. Ah cannie believe it. Danny toppin heesell. He jumped in front o the eleven o'clock train tae Aberdeen. Aye aff the bridge at Magdalen Green. A canny see him daen that but there wis a witness. Aye some wummin saw him dae it. She was wackin her doag."

DONKEYS AND ASSES

Derik Hammond

Bomber was one of those wiry types few dared cross – just a tad over average height, but strong — three years of hard graft at the coal depot had seen to that. Though the pay was nothing to boast about, there were a few customers — personal acquaintances mainly — for whom he added an extra bag or two without registering it in the delivery logbook. Such customers never dared let this favour go unreciprocated, offering cash or barter pilfered from their own places of work as a return of favour.

Bomber moved in circles that brought him into contact with short-skirted city slappers who offered nothing but momentary sexual pleasure yet Bomber was ambitious and capable of better things – or so he thought. To improve his social standing he watched every nature, current affairs, science and history programme on television, absorbing their content with the ease of a top-grade student. Brimming with confidence, he soon found he could impress the well-educated customers in affluent Broughty Ferry with his self-acquired knowledge of — among other subjects — ethics, history, literature and cosmology. He even won over stuck-up Mrs Fraser's admiration when he was able to tell her the current location of the Brinjal Pickle in the 'foods of the world' stock at Tesco's and was rewarded by her asking him to call her Myra.

Yet, despite all his efforts, Bomber orbited the attractive, well-groomed, and well-scented, young women in the Bruach cocktail bar without ever being able to strike up more than a passing word or two with them. And in that he found a certain disappointment in life.

At the other end of Dundee, in a different world, Bomber sat at a table in the Tally bar. He shook his head. Look at him, he thought, gazing at Harry, if someone asked me what animal he was like, it would be a cross between *Homo erectus* and *Equus asinus*. 'Never have I seen a man with a face upon which nature had depicted the character of its owner with such damning perfection.' He felt a surge of satisfaction at the eloquent turn of phrase, though deep down he knew it was not

DONKEYS AND ASSES

entirely an original thought. And where the fuck did he get his money from... a dead aunt? He subdued a smirk as he raised his pint glass, surreptitiously keeping his eye on the smouldering cigarette wedged behind Harry's ear. Harry was ranting on about the great Dundee United players of the past and Bomber did not intend to let Harry's attention wander. He lit up a cigarette and let the smoke screen drift towards Harry. "Malpass—what a player!" he said. The torpedo hit the mark.

"Aye – a great player..." began Harry with puerile enthusiasm.

Bomber rested an elbow on the table, waiting with barely disguised glee as the advancing red front ate into the cigarette paper.

Two minutes later, Harry jumped from his seat, a look of dumb-surprise on his face. From across the table Scarpo, overcome by the comical sight of Harry beating himself about the head, sprayed a mouthful of beer over the ass-faced idiot's trousers.

Bomber plodded through the weeks, always hoping that chance would at last show him a way out of the social cage whose invisible bars might as well have been fashioned from steel. Until, that is, one morning in January. As crystals of frost sparkled under an electric-blue sky, Bomber knocked on the door of a large house set on the hill overlooking Broughty Ferry—a new customer. As the door opened, so did Bomber's mouth—as if about to utter 'coal'—but the word stuck in his throat giving him the appearance of a goldfish that had leapt from its bowl and was gasping for breath. There, right in front of him, stood a young Debbie Harry look-alike wearing nothing but a dressing robe. From within the house came the deep growl of an animal.

"Just ignore Cerebus, he's locked in the kitchen—his bite's much worse than his bark," said the woman in an upper-class English accent.

Bomber laughed heartily though he had heard that quip before, many times.

"I'm so terribly sorry," said the young woman, her fingers twirling a lock of wet, naturally blond hair by her reddening cheek, "I must look such a mess. Ah, you've brought my coal—I do so love an open fire." She wrapped her arms around her body, deepening the cleavage at the vee of the robe's collar. "It's rather cold today."

Bomber made every attempt to make carrying the first of the

50kg sacks to the coal-bunker in the garden appear effortless. After dumping the last official bag, he met the young woman's eyes as he returned to his truck and decided to add an extra bag without expecting any sort of recompense.

The woman smiled coyly as Bomber handed her the bill. "Can I offer you a coffee?"

Bomber gazed into her eyes, their blueness seeming to offer delight beyond imagination. Bomber was about to say, "You fae..." but checked his tongue — this situation demanded a more refined approach. He calmed his nerves. "Are you from Kensington?"

"Close — Chelsea — but how on *earth* can you possibly tell?"

"Oh, I've been around a bit," he lied. In fact, he had noticed a discarded plastic bag from a store in Kensington High Street lying next to the coal bunker. "Yes, I would love a coffee." At that moment, a spark jumped between them — a moment of pure hormonal harmony.

Two weeks on, on a Saturday afternoon, Bomber's stubbly, slightly Slavic-looking face — a legacy of his mother's twenty-minute affair with a one-handed welder from Krakow — stared out from the mirror in his fastidiously kept bathroom. He rubbed his chin and smirked as he spread the Nivea Sensitive shaving foam over his face. "Hard bastard," he said aloud, "and handsome with it." As he shaved, he hummed the melody of the overture to *The Barber of Seville*. He sprayed on a hint of Gucci aftershave and an hour later, as he stood on Stephanie's doorstep as a guest, *She Loves You* was the tune on his lips. He glanced at his fingernails — and removed the last crumb of black grit with his teeth as he waited for the door to open.

As Bomber stepped into Steph's hallway, they stopped to exchange an embrace but her impatient passion got the better of her and Bomber soon found himself in a walk-in shower enclosure with piping hot water flushing over his body — Steph was taking no chances. Then, with Bomber still naked as the day he was born, she led him to a bath towel spread over the bench in the sauna room.

"I find sawnas so invigorating," quipped Bomber as Steph sat beside him."

"It's not *saw*...na," Steph said, correcting Bomber's pronunciation as her snow-white robe dropped from her body, "it's *zow*...na."

Bomber felt his face flush at his mistake but the heat of the

DONKEYS AND ASSES

'zow...na', he hoped, had masked his embarrassment. Casting aside this momentary feeling of inadequacy, Bomber watched the beads of sweat gather on Steph's breasts. Steph smiled, put her arm around his shoulder and landed a luscious kiss on his lips. Soon, in the sweltering heat, happy things happened in the *zow*...na.

And Steph's interest in Bomber wasn't just a rich girl's passing fad. Bomber moved in with her and, dressed in a smart suit and wearing sunglasses whatever the weather, began to take care of all the little 'jobs' that needed done. At first, these were purely benign in nature — deliveries of little packages to big houses, long drives in Steph's spanking new Mercedes M-Class to pick up parcels from contacts in Manchester. Then there was the local work — maintaining the income stream and keeping those who had missed a payment fully informed of their predicament. At last, Bomber felt, he had 'leapt like a salmon' up the social scale — a phrase Harry had surreptitiously drummed into him when boring everyone in the Tally with a description of a headed goal at an inconsequential football match.

One evening, Bomber lay with Cerebus on the rug in front of the blazing open fire while, on the white leather sofa with her legs folded to one side, Steph did her nails. It's funny how love turns to business, thought Bomber. The words in his head echoed with an undertone of nostalgia, hinting that the gains he had made recently had been won at the cost of something lost, something with indefinable but immense value. He missed the banter, the jokes, the slappers... and even Harry. He missed, he was forced to admit to himself, his old life in the Tally.

"It's funny how business turns to love," said Steph, as if reading his mind. "Bomber, you know you're the best thing that's happened in my life. I couldn't have carried on the business without you, you know that."

Bomber looked up to Steph and, subduing the secret melancholy plucking at his heartstrings, smiled. Steph did not lift her gaze from the file that rasped finely across her nails. "Is something wrong?" asked Bomber.

Steph at last lifted her eyes saying, "Darling, there's been a teensy weensy bit of trouble lately. One of the local distributors — you haven't met him yet — a chap with a face like a mule — has been causing a bit of bother. He's worked for me for years. I thought I could rely on him. He'll have to go, I'm afraid."

Bomber stood at the swing doors that were the entrance to the Tally and slowly drew in a lungful of air. He knew that sitting at the usual table would be the same old crowd. In his designer jeans and bespoke German shirt, he knew he would attract attention. But he also knew he would be welcomed like a long lost Joseph the moment his old friends saw him. The door crashed open. A drunken girl staggered into his arms. She looked at him through squinting eyes, her nose almost touching his.

"Hey, hing on a meenit… is that you Bomber? Whaur the fuck hiv ye been?"

As the door recoiled to reveal the inside of the bar, Bomber caught a glimpse of the table where Harry, Dave and Scarpo sat speaking, he surmised, about the same old trash. Time, he had read in a story by Jorge Borges, was a garden of forking paths that could never cross. He turned on his heels and called Steph from his mobile as he headed towards the Mercedes. "I'll see to it, Steph, I promise."

PLEASE LET ME EXPLAIN

Jean Langlands

The cell door clangs shut behind me and I've been left to reflect on my misfortune. How can it be that I, a pillar of the local community, and a long standing member of the Women's Guild, find myself incarcerated in a cell at the local police station? What will the neighbours think, and my friends? They'll be sure to find out. It's bound to be in all the newspapers by tomorrow. I blame him, the bastard.

It was the wedding of the year, at least in our small circle. Two hundred guests attended the ceremony in St. Stephens church and my daughter looked beautiful. Everybody said so and I was so proud of her. I felt wonderful myself in a lovely turquoise dress and jacket with matching hat I'd bought from my favourite department store. The reception was held at a big country house hotel and no expense was spared. It's a pity her father didn't live to see it. He would have been so proud of us all. We danced the night away. My daughter Amy and her husband Darren seemed like the perfect couple. He's the manager of our local garden centre and Amy works for the council planning department.

(Wish he'd stop looking at me through that spyhole. I'm not going to do anything stupid.)

Within a year things had started to go wrong. Darren, it turned out, was seeing someone else. I couldn't believe it but Amy said it was true. She even said she wished she hadn't ditched Max in favour of him. (The words 'frying pan' and 'fire' sprang to mind but, of course, I said nothing.) Apparently, this woman Darren was seeing worked at the same store as him. Well, I just had to go and see what she looked like. I waited until it was the bold boy's day off, then I drove over to the retail park. I hovered around, pretending to be deeply interested in a tray of pink geraniums. She didn't know who I was but I soon sussed her out. She was wearing her name badge, 'Marilyn McCluskey.'

What did Darren see in her? She was not exactly sylph-like and her hair colour, blonde with brown streaks, was definitely out of a bottle. The place was pretty busy so I decided it was better not to confront her.

It was about six months later that Amy and her husband finally split up. He and Marilyn were planning to move to England. Apparently, they'd both got a transfer to a store in Carlisle. Well, good riddance to them. I decided to advertise my wedding outfit for sale. I couldn't bear to look at it now, let alone wear it. I placed an advert in the *Courier* and two people phoned to enquire. The first lady who arrived at the house admired the outfit but thought it wasn't for her. A couple of hours elapsed before the second enquiry. This lady seemed very keen and would be at the house within the hour. A short time later the doorbell rang. Well, when I answered the door I couldn't believe my eyes.

"Hello there," she said. "I've come about the ad."

"It's you."

"Yes, my name is Marilyn... Marilyn McCluskey. I phoned earlier about the ad."

"Oh, I know who you are," I said. "You're the woman who broke up my daughter's marriage."

All my pent up anger exploded and I punched her full on the mouth. She staggered backwards, blood trickling down her chin.

"And you're never a size 14," I shouted as I slammed the door in her face.

He's looking at me again. At last he's opening the cell door. Maybe, I'll get a chance to explain. No, it's dinner on a plastic plate.

"Hello Mrs Fraser, here's some lunch for you and a cup of tea. You seemed to have calmed down a bit."

"Thank you, constable. But when am I getting out of here?"

"You'll be released this afternoon, once the paperwork is done."

"But, what's going to happen to me? I haven't done anything wrong."

"That's up to the courts to decide."

"You mean I could be charged? This is ridiculous."

"It's not down to me. But for your own sake try not to get

PLEASE LET ME EXPLAIN

agitated, and don't argue with the inspector."

That policeman's quite nice really, more than can be said for the macaroni cheese. He says if they decide to charge me I could be up before the sheriff in a few weeks. I ask him which one and he says it could be Sheriff Bannister. My heart skips a beat at this news. You see, Mr Bannister was a member of the Rotary Club when my husband Jim was alive. The two of them got on well and I met the man myself a few times at charity events. He was very nice and is bound to remember me. What a stroke of luck. Now, maybe I could contrive to meet up with him again, or his wife. Yes, that's it. Sybil was lovely and she kind of owes me a favour from way back. She'll put in a good word for me!

Why does time goes by so slowly when you're waiting for an important event? There's been a strange silence from the neighbours, apart from Mrs Connor. She's the lady from two doors down: daft old bat. She pretends to be sympathetic but really she's desperate for news. But my friends have been very nice, especially Sybil Bannister. We met for coffee and I told her the whole story.

"Oh my dear Myra," she said, "sounds like you've had a terrible time."

"Yes, I still can't believe what's happened. I'm hoping you can help me."

"Yes, of course. I'll put you in touch with a very good solicitor. Her name is Anna Smith. I'll write down her number."

"Thank you Sybil, but I was rather hoping you could have a word with your husband on my behalf."

"Well, I'm not supposed to discuss court matters with him."

"Oh dear no, I suppose not. Mind you, my daughter Amy did use her influence at the planning department to get your extension approved. Don't you remember Sybil?"

She seemed taken aback. "Yes indeed you're right," she said.

"And it was, if I remember, rather a large extension with decking all round. In fact, it overlooked your neighbours somewhat."

Sybil looked a bit pained, and began to finger her pearl necklace. "Point taken. One good turn deserves another," she agreed.

"Exactly!"

"I'll have a word with Nigel."

Jean Langlands

"Thank you, Sybil. Now let me pay for these coffees. It's been lovely to see you again."

It's been a long wait but today's the day. I didn't think they would actually charge me, but it seems that Marilyn is determined to testify against me. She's a bitch. Darren's got what he deserves. My solicitor, the one Sybil recommended, says it would be very hard to prove the case as there are no witnesses. She says I'm sure to get off. It's Marilyn's word against mine. The police have no evidence. And, she says, it's in my favour that I've never been in trouble before.

It's awful sitting here in the sheriff court waiting my turn to go in. Amy has come with me to give me moral support. There are some really weird folk hanging around. God knows what they've done. Probably beaten up their wives or assaulted someone. There's so much violence nowadays.

I just don't believe it, there's Mrs Connor sitting over there, probably come to gloat. I give her a nod but for some reason she looks away.

Then it's my turn. They're calling my name.

Well, that's that then. It's bad enough that Sheriff Bannister isn't here. Called away unexpectedly it seems. How convenient.

Marilyn has had her say and I've had mine and the replacement sheriff looks unimpressed. I suppose it's all in a day's work for him.

Then suddenly they've got a witness. Mrs Connor is being sworn in. The old besom. So that's why she's here.

"Yes your worship," she says, "I saw it all."

"Tell us in your own words Mrs Connor what you saw that day."

She gives a little cough, looks at me then back to the judge.

"It was a nice sunny day and I happened to be in my garden, doing a bit of weeding when I heard this commotion going on…"

It's a two hundred pound fine and a warning to be on my best behaviour. It could be worse, I suppose, and I could appeal. That Mrs Connor is as deaf as a post. How could she have heard anything from two doors down?

As for Sybil Bannister, she was no help at all. I'll strike her of my list of friends… yes, definitely.

A CLAUSE FOR CONCERN

Paul Sykes

His arms, tanned and tattooed, pump twenty pound dumbbells, sweat trickles down his contorted face. His perfect white teeth are gritted, his neck muscles flexed. He blows out heavily, then swings his arms out to the side and pumps the weights in towards his ears. His pecs rip and the nipples…

Max opens his eyes. He takes a moment to focus, as if suffering from an attack of vertigo. His iPhone is strumming away and he reads the message: 'Take the pink one now.' Max reaches into the mini pharmacy in his desk, takes a pill and washes it down with a slug of Evian. All the time his mind is racing.

"Max… Max… Max!"

He looks up to see his PA, Cheryl, standing in the door of his office, immaculately dressed though it's still only 7.30.

"Your wife is holding on line three." She was about to turn then said, "Oh and Neville wants the team in the Board Room in ten minutes, no excuses."

Max feels a wave of panic just at the mention of that name… Neville. With his heart rate increasing he takes a deep breath and picks up the phone.

"Rebekah, Meine Liebling." He's tired and has forgotten that they had agreed to speak German only when they were in Germany or visiting his family in Zurich. Normally they picked a neutral language like Spanish.

"Max, you have got to stop doing this. I cannot cope and I need you home." Her tone is steely. "The twins are driving me to distraction. I have been up all night and you're in some hotel… it's not fair." The tone changes and she starts to cry.

"Rebekah, this deal is four days from completion. We complete in Essen on Thursday and then we can go to Zurich for a couple of weeks. Mama and Papa are excited to meet the boys." He can hear her stifle sniffles down the phone.

"I'm so lonely... I shouted at James last night... he's six weeks old... I'm... I'm a bad mother."

"No you are not. No one ever tells you what parenthood is really like, not like doing your job." Max can see Cheryl reappear at the door and tap her watch in that irritating school-ma'am way she has. "Look I have to go. I'll call later tonight. Give my love to Jamie and Rupe." Max hangs up as Rebekah stops stifling the sniffles and starts to cry again.

Max looks out of the window from his 25th floor eyrie. What is it about snow in London that is just depressing and yet in Zurich is so appealing? Max stands, puts on his jacket, straightens his tie, flicks his cuffs, flattens what is left of his thinning hair, and stretches his gangly six foot two frame. He picks up a portfolio from his desk and drags his weary body out of the office. He nods to someone across the room and half a dozen bodies rise from desks and make to follow him to the Board Room.

The room is abuzz. There are about twenty people milling around, brokers and bankers, talking on mobiles, drinking coffee, drawing on over-sized post-it notes on the walls. The large glass table is swamped with legal books, reports and laptops. At the centre stands Neville immaculately groomed and bossing someone down the phone.

"Fuck it and fuck him. Just a minute – Swiss Tony's here." He looks at Max. "We good on the remuneration clauses?" Max nods.

"It's the mutt's nuts," Neville barks down the telephone line. "We'll have the Krauts bleeding from the eyeballs by Friday." He hangs up.

Max winces. He knows that everything that is good in Neville's world is the 'dog's ballocks' or the 'mutt's nuts' and everything bad is 'screwing the pooch'. What is it about the English and their dogs, he thinks. However Max knows not to cross Neville: this is a man educated at the Jimmy Goldsmith school of Doing Business, who now advises the Chicago Board of Trade and who has been called in by Goldman Sachs to head up this deal. If anything personifies capitalism red in tooth and claw it is the dapper, small, foul-mouthed Neville.

Neville calls the meeting to order and his myrmidons assemble round the table. "Swiss Tony is going to update us on the remuneration clause in a sec. Hugh, PR."

A CLAUSE FOR CONCERN

Max sees the rep from the financial PR company start his report. "The Germans are reeling on all fronts. They're fighting hard to deal with accusations of failing to protect shareholder interests. Several big German dailies and financial websites are giving them a good kicking… with a little prompting from us. A straw poll of major corporate investors looks like swaying our way. Their unions are up in arms as well."

Max watches as the vulpine Neville relishes each turn of the screw, each ratchet notch, each throw of the dice coming up six. He feels increasingly uneasy about the whole under-the-radar nature of this takeover.

Neville turns to his chief hatchet man: "Steve, paint me the future."

Steve – Stephen Brooks-Myler of the Oxfordshire Brooks-Mylers – begins his report: "I have been discussing various scenarios with our economists at the bank and we believe that, ultimately, our client can have the pick of the divisions they want, at a price set by us of course, and then we can break up the whole conglomerate and potentially make in excess of six billion dollars over the asking price."

There are a couple of low wolf whistles and Neville licks his lips the way Caligula might before tucking into a lightly roasted proconsul. This is what is making Max so uneasy. The whole operation has gone rogue. Even the client, a small but ambitious UK Pharma group, is in play and he is not at all sure that his law firm and the bank has any real knowledge of what Neville and his crew are up to.

Neville's first words to them had been,"We're going to the mattresses people." Max had to have the reference explained to him. Apparently it was all about going to war in secret so here they all were exiled to the Marriot in West India Quay with its sultry views over Poplar. At least it's only five minutes walk away from the building they are currently sitting in. A few tumultuous years ago it had belonged to Lehman Brothers. Everyone here is on secondment and on the QT and the moment the deal is done they will go back to their day jobs.

"Listen up, people, we are really close. We have most of the shares and money in place. Max, can you take us through the remuneration clause. We need it watertight. Once the Krauts accept the deal, we're going tear in to them like the Securities and Exchange Commission looking for Dick Fuld's expenses."

Neville – the maestro of financial mayhem – nods to Max. Max stands and starts on his report. He can see Neville passing notes to Steve and passing quizzical looks to other members of his financial cadre. Max's thoughts drift to when he first came to London and his first case representing Iconic Branding, and to his old friend Marcus, who hired him. Lucky old Marcus now running his own business and beholden to no one, least of all slime like Neville.

Max is back in his office. He tosses the contract on the desk and closes his eyes. His mind is immediately a whirl of conflicting thoughts. The deal, Neville's duplicity, and Rebekah and the boys… He imagines his family in Zurich happy in his parents' garden. Not like the fraught and tense days and nights in Dulwich since the boys were born.

"Max. Max, are you asleep?"

Max eases one eye open to see Neville's grape-coloured face two inches from his. "No, Neville, I am merely reviewing some of the finer points of the contract." He indicates the sheaf of papers spread out on the desk.

"Just checking. Marunchak thinks it's still a bit shit – the detail on the remuneration clause."

"Really, and he is an expert in Germanic business law?"

"Don't get funny with me, you proxy Kraut. The whole thrust of this deal is that they destroyed shareholder value for their own gain; there can be no sweetheart deals. They must be punished and seen to be punished."

"That is not true, Neville. We are destroying them for our own…"

"Truth and perception – not the same thing!" snaps Neville.

"Does the client know we are going to screw them on the sale of assets?" Max glares at Neville.

"Fuck 'em, nothing more than a bunch of jumped up chemists, good for a handful of Strepsils and fuck all else. Get the contract nailed. I have to hop in a cab and take the team to Aston's for some Krug and fish paste."

Neville ducks out of the door; Max winces for the umpteenth time. Neville thinks expensive and good taste are one and the same.

Max walks into the Hotel gym. It's nearly nine and the place is practically deserted. The contract has been agreed. Everything will now go to print and they will assemble in the lounge of their executive jet hire company on Thursday. Max starts the machine on a gentle jog and starts pacing.

A CLAUSE FOR CONCERN

Over in the far corner he can see a man pumping free weights, his broad shoulders bursting through the cut off vest. Their eyes meet fleetingly. Max stares at the pedometer of the machine. His heart is racing; he cranks up the speed. He glances again at the man in the corner, his eyes filled with raw aggression as he pumps out the reps and the veins in his arm stand out like a road map of Italy. Their eyes meet again and Max smiles wanly at him.

The muscle man suddenly dashes across the gym and grabs Max by his t-shirt. "I'm not a fucking bender you fucking bender." Oscar Wilde he certainly isn't. And, with that, he relentlessly pummels Max with all his might.

Max lies in the hospital bed. A couple of police officers stand next to him. One hands him a piece of paper. "That has the incident number, consult your solicitor. Three broken ribs, a fractured cheek bone, broken nose and suspected concussion – that is assault and battery. Let me know how you want to proceed." They turn and leave.

Seconds later Max looks up and sees Rebekah standing there, pram and twins in tow. He smiles and he can see the relief on her face. She comes to sit next to him.

"Honey, I need you to do something for me." Max reaches into the bedside table and pulls out his hotel key.

Two days later Max walks into the lounge of the executive jet company. The right side of his face is puffed and swollen and a mix of livid red and black has blurred the vision in his partially closed right eye. Neville and his elite Praetorian guards look up at him as he strides in.

Neville acknowledges what has been buzzing round the office. "Nice shiner! You should beware. These power lifters are all closet cases." With that Neville turns to his team and gives them his version of a pep talk: "Okay, men, lock and load, hands off cocks and hands on socks. Time to man up and give the Boche a bit more of what they got in 1945." He turns and leads them out to the cars that will take them to the waiting jet.

Max is quietly consulting his laptop when there is an explosion of rage from the front of the plane. Neville is striding down the plane waving his iPhone. "Who the fuck knows about this?" Steve and the Pretorian guards cluster around him trying to find out what is going on. "Breaking on *The Telegraph* website… the entire deal… fucking everything… my bonus… quotes from the client… the whole shebang!"

One of the team shouts: "*The Guardian* has got it too. Fuck, they're attributing it to WikiLeaks."

Neville's face manages to go an even deeper shade of purple. "You fuckers, I want your phone records, your emails! One of you is a Judas and I will find you and tear your fucking heart out."

At that moment, Neville's phone rings. "Mr Blankfein…what? I can turn it around. It's the British press, bottom feeders… what *The Times* and *The Post*, Mother…." Neville hangs up. "Tell the pilot we're returning to Heathrow."

Max calmly picks up his phone: "Hola cariña…"

FUTURE SENSE

Amanda Barclay

Marcus considered the cover of *Business Briefing*. He had to admit his photo looked pretty sharp. There he was leaning against his desk wearing a black polo and an expression of grave authority. The office looked beyond amazing too. That floor-to-wall fish tank had been well worth the wrangle with the halfwit plumber. Recessed lighting provided a dramatic counterpoint to the muted earth tone walls. The slate floor had cost a fortune but provided the perfect finishing touch. The cover was captioned 'What next for Future Sense?' – what next indeed?

Marcus had explained his business vision to the interviewer. "More than ever in uncertain times people want to know what the future holds – and do you know why that is? So they can prepare for it. Future Sense recognises that desire and provides the next generation in fortune telling. Not only do we offer top psychic talent, but based on the readings we add our unique additional life coaching element."

The reporter had asked where the idea for the business had come from but on that matter he had been a little vague implying it was more of a life calling than a business idea. He could hardly say it was all down to his Aunt Pat in Dundee. He had been working with Iconic Branding at the time and would stay over with her whenever he had a business trip north. On one particular occasion he had arrived at the house to find a group of Pat's friends ensconced in the living room, chattering excitedly like noisy starlings.

Pat pulled him in. "Tea will be a bit late tonight, Mark. Leon's coming to give us a reading."

He had given up trying to get Aunt Pat to call him Marcus.

"Didn't know you were in a book group," he said as he took off his coat.

"Don't be daft! He's coming to read our fortunes."

At this juncture a chubby man in a flamboyant shirt bustled in.

"Evening, girls. Yes, it's me, Leon, King of the Gypsies, large as life and twice as lovely!" He acknowledged the ladies with wide smiles and small fluttering waves.

His first customer shuffled through to the dining-room. "Keep your fingers crossed he sees a tall dark stranger in my cards," she giggled.

While they waited Pat explained how it worked. "Leon reads your cards and other things – not cheap but he's the best. Last time he was here, Hazel took in her late mum's wedding ring. Leon told her things about her mother that there's no way anyone else could have known."

"How much does he charge?" Marcus asked curiously

"£30 a reading."

Marcus looked round the room swiftly and did the sums: twelve heads at £30 a pop. £360. Not bad for a short night's work. No overheads and you could bet HMRC saw none of the proceeds.

He continued to muse on this but became aware he was being questioned by a small stout lady wedged in the opposite armchair.

"So, ye're still workin in sales, are ye son?"

He smiled condescendingly

"Not really. I'm a brand consultant actually." She looked baffled so sighing inwardly he elaborated. "You know – Lucozade?"

She considered the question and answered slowly, "Eh. But eh'd never drink it. Eh'm no a great wan fir fizzy pop, bangs me right up… As a metter o fact…"

He cut across her smartly.

"It used to be a drink for people in hospital – *Lucozade aids recovery.*"

"Oh, eh mind o't. It came in yellae cellophane. Richt cheery, it wis. When eh visited meh…"

He continued undaunted. "Well now it's a sports drink for athletes. That transformation was brought about by repositioning the offer and…"

"Still full of sugar and gas though."

Keeping the edge out his voice he said, "And that's where brand consultants come in. People consider the product in a whole new way."

She looked utterly unimpressed. "Sounds like new soles, old boots," she sniffed. "Onywey, eh'm up next," and hauling herself out the chair, she limped into the dining-room.

FUTURE SENSE

Marcus watched as the ladies came back after their readings. Some were full of self-importance and bursting to tell. Others came back slowly and deep in contemplation. Marcus guessed dead relatives had been contacted, or worries had been addressed. Indeed Mrs Lucozade was busy telling Pat about the red aura Leon had sensed at the top of her leg.

"He asked if eh'd hud a pain – ye ken eh've bin plagued. Onywey, he predicted an operation wid be the pathway to freedom. Funny thing is Dr Lewis sayed a hip replacement might be an option. Meh, Leon is amazing!"

Leon's dulcet tones trilled through from the dining-room. "Any more for any more?"

Marcus stood up and to all the ladies' astonishment strolled into the dining-room. "Think I'll have a go."

As Marcus entered Leon started and hastily threw a black silk scarf over the pile of ten pound notes he had been deftly counting.

"Come away in. I don't get many gentleman callers but you're very welcome, son, all the same."

Leon's sharp eyes ever so casually scanned Marcus's appearance as he began in a sing-song voice, "I see offices, lots of computers. Now let me see are you in a professional field maybe?"

Leon left the phrase hanging. Marcus let it hang.

"Now you used to quarrel with a family member when you were young but now you are reconciled. Was it your father?"

Marcus steepled his fingers. "You're the fortune teller. You tell me."

A look of irritation passed over Leon's face. He regrouped and injecting a sorrowful note into his voice intoned, "You still miss your grandad."

"He's still alive."

"Ah, that's it. You don't get to see as much of him as you'd like."

Marcus sat back and looked at Leon appraisingly. "The thing is, Leon – is that even your real name? So far you've told me nothing I don't already know or that anyone with half a brain could guess."

"The ways of the spirits are not our ways. I'm just a channel, a conduit if you like…"

"Leon, you know what? I think you are good at what you do – reading people, leading questions, telling folk what they want to hear… But you're no fortune teller, are you?"

Leon looked at him with loathing; the arch playful demeanour had evaporated completely. "Okay, Okay. I admit Leon is a bit of fun for the ladies. If I turned up as plain Len it wouldn't be the same. But the fortune telling? That's the real deal. I do have the sight – my mother was known for her predictions. I wouldn't muck about with this stuff. You've got to respect it."

Marcus reached for the pile of cards and selecting one, handed it to Leon. Leon glanced at it and replaced it in the deck, saying nothing.

"So what does it say?" Marcus demanded.

"I think it would be better that I don't read your cards."

"Oh, come on!"

Leo shook his head obstinately and began packing his cards away.

Marcus persisted. "So what did you see?"

"Changes – and don't get involved with things you don't understand," Leon said curtly.

Marcus reached for his wallet. "£30 I believe?" he said, throwing the notes on the table.

Leon met his eyes. "There's nothing to pay."

It seemed Leon was a better fortune teller than Marcus had given him credit for. The following week Iconic Branding announced wide-scale redundancies. Marcus was a casualty. He was not overly dismayed. He had always wondered about setting up his own business. All it required was one brilliant idea. Not hard for a man of his creative abilities. Coolly he assessed his options. When there was a recession on, what did people really need? They needed money. Fastidiously he dismissed the obvious – pawnbrokers, cash for gold. How about something more esoteric? Career coaching? Surely that had to be money for old rope.

For some reason his thoughts kept returning to Leon and that fat pile of tenners. His mind began to click. In hard times people did worry about the future. Wasn't that what fortune tellers offered? Benign reassurance? The real problem with fortune tellers was their image – downmarket and dodgy. What fortune telling needed was a revamp and who better to do it?

Marcus undertook some extensive research on basic human psychology. He already knew that although people considered themselves unique their concerns were universal. It wasn't rocket

FUTURE SENSE

science. He decided fortune telling not only needed a makeover but also more oomph. He came up with the concept of fortune telling with a life coaching aspect. Suitably woolly. He would get others to do the readings which would be enhanced by some surreptitious background checks. Finally Marcus took a course in lifestyle coaching. Consultations could be done in person or remotely via Skype. Franchising was a distinct possibility. Future Sense had launched and soon went exponential. As he had said to *Business Briefing* there was something about Future Sense that really resonated with the current zeitgeist.

Reluctantly, Marcus laid the article aside. Quickly checking his online calendar, he realised he had a new client coming in at 11am – a guy called Nick something or other. This was good news. He was definitely capturing the previously untapped male market.

Suddenly the office door opened and a small dark man entered noiselessly.

Marcus looked up. "Can I help you?"

"I have an appointment at 11.00."

"Oh, was there no-one in reception?" Marcus would need to have a stern word with his receptionist.

"Anyway come in Mr…? My apologies, I don't appear to have your surname."

"I didn't give it," the man said firmly and sat down uninvited.

His attitude irritated Marcus – but he said silkily, "Of course. So many of my high profile clients do prefer a measure of anonymity."

The man's sudden appearance had disrupted his usual client preparation "Now let's get your file up." Marcus frowned at the screen.

"That's strange. I don't appear to have received the briefing from your initial session with my colleague."

"Are you sure?" The man had a mellifluous voice and an unplaceable accent. "You should perhaps look again."

Sure enough, just left of his cursor was the file. Marcus could have sworn it was not there a second ago.

"The key theme from your reading was your career concerns. A downfall early in your working life has left you questioning the validity of your current role. Shall we explore that?"

"I think I would prefer to talk about you. You seem very successful." Here the man indicated the magazine cover.

Marcus didn't like the man's sarcastic tone nor how this session was shaping up but he attempted a modest moue.

"Success doesn't just happen; it takes a lot of work."

"Some people might say what you do here at Future Sense is a little presumptuous. I mean telling people's fortune is one thing but then advising them what to do? That could be viewed as meddling with destiny."

Marcus felt a prickle of unease. He suspected this client was not what he seemed. An undercover reporter perhaps? "Well, if helping people could be said to be presump..."

The man continued, "There are those who think that you shouldn't dabble with things you don't understand."

Marcus suddenly saw red. "Now look here, Nick, or whoever the hell you are. You've no idea what you are talking about. Why don't you get out before I throw you..."

The sudden disappearance of the founder of Future Sense was the cause of endless speculation in the press. He had last been seen in his office. Other than a peculiar scorch mark on the slate floor there was nothing to indicate anything untoward had happened. There was talk of bright candles burning fast.

It seemed an ignominious end when *Business Briefing* featured the state-of-the-art Future Sense offices with the headline, 'Closed due to unforeseen circumstances'.

REMEMBERING JAY

Elizabeth Taylor

Did ye see thon on the telly the ither nicht? The lad wha wis blawin intae bits o plumber's pipe an it soondit jist like the Caird Hall organ? Meh, whit daft weys some fowk think o tae spend thir time!

Me? Eh've nivir bin wan fir hoabies. Och, when Eh wis wee Eh used tae collect Typhoo tea cairds an aw they things. But noo? Well, Eh suppose Eh wid hae tae say meh favourite things are a bit o windae shoppin an gaun tae funerals. No a graveside, mind you. It's aye ower cauld. But thir's somethin special aboot a richt guid send-aff, whether it's the Kirk or the Crem, especially as meh pal Agnes, her that works in the charity shop, ayways sees tae it that Eh look the pairt. Eh jist like the smell o the lilies, aw the braw music, an the restful feel o the place, if ye ken whit Eh mean. And ye aften get asked fir a wee cup o tea efter.

Eh ken aw the words aff beh hairt. Eh think fowk are aye pleased thir's somebody there wha kens the hymns an sings oot, ...*in pa-astures green*, *Simply the best!*, *Eh'm luvvin angels instead*.

That wis wan they chose fir pair Jay last week. Eh dinnae think it wis richt. No in the circumstances. It widnae hae bin meh choice, but there again, she wisnae meh lassie.

It wis that sad. Jist a couple o rows filled, an maistly auld fowk at that. Eh wis only there beh chance, ye ken. But they aye say things are meant.

It had been a richt dreich mornin, an seein Eh'd naethin else tae dae, Eh taen the Number Wan an endit up at the Crematorium door jist as the hearse wis arrivin. Eh sat doon at the back as usual. Bein on noddin acquaintance wi the attendant, he passed me the Order o Service. Eh recognised her straicht awa frae the pictir on the front o it, even tho the photae had bin taen years ago. She looked sae happy. And bonnie. But she wis a bonnie lass, deep doon.

Eh got a richt shock, Eh kin tell ye. Wha'd hae thocht it? Well, meh heed wis swimmin. Eh thocht o aw the times oor paths hud crossed.

Elizabeth Taylor

The memories cam floodin back. An aw the time, meh lugs wir strainin tae hear whit the meenister wis sayin, fir the service had startit. Eh wis tryin tae find oot whit had happened tae her, pair sowl.

"*Friends, we gather here today to remember Jessica Maria Patterson…*"

Jessica? Jessica? She telt me she wis cried Jay. Mebbe she didnae like her richt name an cheenged it. Fowk aye seem tae shorten things nooadays. Jay suited her better onywey, nae doot aboot that. Eh suppose beh richts it should hae been Jigh, but there ye are.

"*… daughter to Joseph and Mary…*"

It soondit like she wis some relation o Christ himsel! A fallen angel she certainly wis. Eh looked at the pair o them, sittin aw po-faced. Eh thocht, she didnae hae muckle time fir them, an they sure as Hell hadnae time fir her, judgin beh the wey she wis treated.

There they wir, sittin beh thirsels richt doon the front. The mither seemed tae be squeezin a hankie in her haunds, like she wis aboot tae strangle it. She looked nether tae left nor richt, but sat there wi her een on the coffin, jist starin an starin like she couldnae tak it aw in. The faither wis tall an thin wi a bald patch, an he sat that straicht, like he wis wearin a surgical corset. If ye'd seen him in the street, ye micht hae sayed he wis kind o distinguished lookin – like he wis a professor or somethin. But Eh ken better. Fowk like him should be locked up.

"*… a tormented soul, now at rest…*"

Well, Eh thocht, she sure hud a rought time o't. But Eh'm no gonnae mak excuses fir her. Thon time in the Overgate'll stey wi me aw ma days.

Eh'd jist been tae the lavvie an Eh went tae wash ma haunds. Eh've a wee touch o arthritis, an see tae get watter oot o thon taps! Eh tried an tried an eventually Eh pit meh bag doon on the flair an used the twa haunds thegither, wan on tap o the ither, tae shove the damn thing doon. Of coorse, beh the time Eh'd gotten the skoosh o soap an rinsed it aff, meh bag wis awa – messages, keys, purse, bus pass, the lot. Thon spey mannie at Pat's certainly hidnae forecast thon!

The place wis busy. It wis a Setterday. But of coorse, naebody'd seen onything. Eh wis in a richt state, Eh kin tell ye. Well, a wifie felt sorry fir me an gied me the bus fare hame, an beh luck Annie next door wis in. She's got meh spare key. So it wisnae as bad as it micht hae been. But it taen me weeks tae get ower the shock – and save up again tae pey the gas.

Well, it wisnae lang till Eh fund oot wha'd taen meh bag. Eh

REMEMBERING JAY

wis staunin at the bunker lookin oot the kitchen windae wan mornin no lang efter, when Eh noticed a flash o' pink an tartan dashin awa fae meh front door. Beh the time Eh'd gaen tae see wha it wis, there wis naebody there. But, blow me, wis meh bag no lyin there on the step! Nae purse, of coorse. But awthin else – even meh hoose keys. Whaever it wis must o fund the address fae the gas bill an felt guilty.

A couple o weeks efter Eh wis in the Wellgate. Eh'd been up in the Reference readin the Announcements in the *Courier* an Eh spehed a lassie hingin aboot outside the lavvies – a lassie wi bright pink hair, a wee black leather jaicket held thegither wi preens, an a wee bit tartan skirt that scarce covered her backside.

Eh sat doon outside The Weavers, like Eh wis waitin fir a cuppie, an watched. The lassie went intae the lavvies wi naethin an cam oot wi a BHS cerrier bag. Eh wid hae recognised thon hair onywhere.

Eh dinae ken whit cam ower me. Eh wis that share it wis her. Eh went ower an stuck meh airm oot tae stop her frae runnin doon the stairs. "Excuse me, Hen," Eh sayed. "Are you the wan wha taen meh bag in the Overgate lavvies?" Eh think she wis that taen aback, she drapped the bag she wis huddin an ran awa intae the Family History bit.

Well, Eh follaed her an met her at thon funny gate-like doors. "Eh ken it wis you," Eh sayed. "An ye're still at it. Takin bags fae pair bodies wha can ill afford it. Ye shid be ashamed o yirsel."

Eh wis expectin her tae rin aff again, but she didnae. She started tae greet. She grat an she grat an she grat until her hale body wis shakin. "There, there, Hen" Eh sayed, an Eh taen her beh the airm, still greetin, alang tae The Weavers an boucht her a cup o'tea.

Eh dinnae ken if it wis relief at bein fund oot or whit, but wance she startet tae talk she wis like a drippin tap. Eh couldnae get her tae stop. Me, an auld wifie fae Douglas, an her, a punk-like lassie wi a posh accent, pourin oot her life history like there wis nae tomorra.

Jay, she tellt me her name wis. Jay frae Lochee. She tellt me aw aboot how naebody seemed tae unnerstaund. How sh'd gotten intae drugs when she wis still at the High School. How her mither had pit her oot. An her faither! Well! On an on an on she went, until she'd nae mair tae say.

Well, Eh could only dae whit onybody wid dae bein tellt aw thon. Eh pit meh airms roond her an held her an rocked her like she wis a bairn. Then, athoot anither word, she stade up, squeezed ma haund, an walked awa. Eh watched her gawn doon the steps, thinkin pair, pair lass.

Eh met Jay a puckle o times in the toon efter that. Wance Eh taen her tae The Deep Sea an treated her tae a fish supper. She wisnae a bad lassie. No deep doon. Mind you, some o the things she sayed wid mak yer hair curl... It wis like it wis a relief tae her haein somebody tae listen.

"...*Lost to us in such tragic circumstances*..."

O, meh God, Eh thocht. O, meh God. Dinnae tell me she wis the wan Eh'd read aboot in the paper. It wis even on the wireless. They'd hud tae shut the Brig fir aboot twa oors. The lifeboat wis oot fae the Ferry an awthin, but they wir ower late. It didnae say wha jamp of coorse. It never dis.

"...*may she find eternal peace*..."

Well, she's awa tae a better place noo. Nae drugs. Nae thievin. Nae pesterin. Nae pretendin. An nae faimly – except fir the angels, an Eh'm share they're lookin efter her richt. The pair, pair lass.

Beh the time the service wis ower, Eh kent whit Eh hud tae dae. Like eyeways, the faimly – whit thir wis o'them – wir aw lined up at the door. Eh jined the queue tae gang oot, hingin back as best Eh could.

The mither still had her hankie gripped in her left haund, but her een wir bone dreh. She never sayed a word tae onybody, but hud oot her richt haund fir shakin.

When it wis meh turn, the faither thanked me fir comin and held oot his haund. Eh moved forrit like Eh wis aboot tae shak his, but instead, Eh grabbed hud o his thingymajig an squeezed it atween meh nails as hard as Eh could, an whispered in his lughole, "Ye filthy bastert. Hell's ower guid fir the likes o you."

He sooked in air atween his teeth. He never sayed a word, but the look in his een wis enough tae tell me the pair lass had been richt.

Then Eh made meh wey oot tae get meh bus. What Eh done widnae mak a scrap o difference tae pair Jay, but beh God it made me feel a Hell o a lot better.

Onywey, Eh'd better shift. Eh'm awa doon the toon fir the Remembrance service at the Steeple Kirk, but Eh'll mak share Eh'm back in time tae see thon lad wi the pipe organ. He'll get meh vote again the nicht.

" *Abide with me*..."

CHARITY FIRST

Jane O'Neill

Cooee! Pat! Izzie! It's me, Agnes. Ehm back fae mi stint in the Ferry branch. Bet yir baith dehin ti hear mi stories. Well, gies a meenit till eh git mi coat aff. Hiv eh got stories! Ane o you twa mak a cup o tea furst, and then eh'll tell yoos aboot 'meh pal Senga' fae Charity First in the Ferry, Oooooo!

Well, yi ken eh wis lookin fir a wee bit extrae money, so when Mrs Carruthers telt me aboot the shifts goin spare in the Ferry shop, eh jumped at the chance o a cupla dayz doon there. Eh thought it might be a cooshee number! Senga is the wummin in charge – eh kent her name wis Senga afore she telt me, as she hid ane o they gold necklaces danglin aroond her neck wi the initials, S E N G A. Eh thought, eh wonder whit Pat and Izzie would say if eh bought ane o they necklaces and ca'd mesel Senga instaid o Agnes!

Now, Senga is big, if ye get mi drift. Big shidders, big fais caked in make-up, and big hair – pushed back wi ane o they hairbands wi the floo'er on the side. So in eh went Wensday mohrnen – right ti the back shop whaur a the bags were stacked up, and met Senga – wis she pleased ti see me? Naa! Speak aboot a fais like the Dundee Fortnight!

Eh said ti her, "Di yi waant me ti start on ane o the bags?"

But no, she grabs the bag oot mi hand and says eh could start dustin the shelves oot the front. There were loadsa bags ti open and eh hid been lookin forward ti a raik among the claes, but eh soon fund oot how she wanted me ti dust!

There eh wis, goin roond the shelves clearin awa the stoor wi ane o they yella dusters – but keepin mi eh on Senga in the back shop. She wis taakin the claes oot the bags and hingin them on a coupla rails, just like we dae here in the Lochee shop. Only, she wis taakin certain frocks and tops and skirts and hingin them on anither rail at the back o the room. There wisna a Rag Pen in sight, so yi ken me, eh went inta the back shop and asked Senga whit she wis daen wi a the claes.

Jane O'Neill

"I'm hanging the stock up to air, Agnes," she says, "then I'll use the steamer to press them and then they'll be ready for the front shop."

She put on ane o they smarmy looks, so eh glowered at her and said, "Ok, keep yir hair on, you dae it your weh and eh'll dae it meh weh! But whit aboot them?" eh says, and pointed ti the ither claes.

"Well, some of the stock needs careful handling, you know. I can spot quality when I see it, and anyway, I may want to purchase some of these goods myself. Staff are awarded twenty per cent discount you know."

"Well," eh says, "in the Lochee shop, we usually keep the good stuff for the windae! If it's a pitcher or a bit o pott'ry it gits sent aff tae Enbra ti get valued. Mrs Carruthers says if the good stuff is in the windae, the punters will come in looking fir mair and that's how yi get regulars that gie good money fir stuff."

"Hmmpf," she says, "all the goods handed in to the Ferry shop are of the best quality. That's why we don't have a Rag Pen as you put it – but some things are better than others I have to say, and actually, I have spotted some very nice dresses that I will consider buying. My grandson is to be Christened on Sunday and I'm looking at some of the designer pieces."

Wi the dustin done, eh offered ti go through the box o bric a brac and again *oor* Senga grabs the box and picks oot a couple o wee gless squirrels – oad lookin things they were – wi big bug ehs, and ane o they queer-looking teddies.

"These squirrels are Russian, Agnes," she says, "and quite collectable." She puts them oot the road on the tap o the shelf. "And this teddy," she huds it up beh the lug, "is a Stieff bear."

"Aw ehh!" Eh says. "Righty ho!" The scabby-lookin bear went on the tap shelf tae.

Next it wis the books, which as you baith ken is meh favourite. Boxes and boxes o books had ti be unloaded and again the bizum wouldna let me get on wi it.

"Put the price labels on the Cornwells and Grishams and Steels, and put them out front straight away, and I'll have a look through the Penguins," she says.

Some o the Penguins, as she ca'd them, were a toarn and mankay, but she kept them aside and eh spotted her flickin through them and pilin them up in a wee coarner. Ney flehs on me, so eh asked

CHARITY FIRST

her whit she wanted wi a pile o toarn books.

She hid this maddenin wy o lookin at yi wi her ehs closed and stickin her chin up, and she goes, "Agnes, you have to be vigilant as to what comes into the shop. Some of these Penguin books are very rare, and collectable, so I like to separate them from the other paperbacks. I have customers who come in specially to buy Penguins."

"Yeh right!" Eh says ti mesel! "Eh've got you clocked."

Anyhow, she then says she is goin ti lunch and meetin a friend in the Willows, so eh says, "Eh'll just bide in the shop and hae the rest o the macaroni peh eh got oot o Greggs."

Eh shut the door efter her and turned the sign ti Closed. Eh perched mesel on the chair at the coonter, and took a wee nosey at the baubles and beads in the gless case. Some guid pearls and earrings mind you, and plenty brooches which are no meh thing, but bonnie a the same.

Eh took a wee gander in the draar. Oh meh! Eh haals oot a lacy bra and sussies! Powder blue wi that diamonte stuff instid o buttons. Eh raiked a bit further and fund mair! Eh checked the sez o the naughties, and thought, nae chance o oor Senga getting inta a 34B! Mair like 44b ah back!

But, meh nose wis getting the better o me so eh trotted through ti the back shop ti check oot the designer claes. Eh'll tell yi there wis some bonnie stuff there and eh spotted a brah winter jeckit and hid anither look at the label: J A E G E R – ye remember the really dear shop that used ti be in Reform Street – naebody bought fae it, and it closed doon! So eh flicked through the rail and clocked the labels, Laura Ashley, Vera Vanstone, Country Casuals, and of coorse the Jaeger jeckit.

It wis past ane o'clock so eh opened the shop and there wis this wummin waitin ti come in. "Oh!" She says, and looks me up and doon. "I'm looking for Senga."

"Sorry, Senga's oot ti lunch. Can eh help?"

"I don't think so," she goes, and pats baith sides o her hair. "I prefer to deal with Senga personally. Tell her Daphne Lefèvre called."

She glared inta the back shop as if she didnae believe is, then turned and marched oot the the shop. Obviously ane o Senga's 'special customers'. Eh didna dare think which Penguin she wis efter! Mind you she did hae the Country Casual look aboot er. Good riddance if yi ask me.

Then anither wummin came in, she waandered aroond, no

Jane O'Neill

really lookin at stuff, so eh says ti her, "Can eh help yi wi anything?"

She wis a bit queer-like, as though she hid somethin ti say but wis fared ti say it. So eh went back ti the coonter. She comes over and says, "I'm looking for dresses, particular dresses."

So eh says, "Any special colour?"

"No, No!" she says, "I'll know them when I see them, you see it's my sister ..."

Anyhow, eventually Senga comes back, ah flushed, and eh can tell twa glesses o wine when eh see it.

"Nice lunch, Senga?" Eh says, and she goes straight inta the back shop. Eh sits whaur eh am, rappin meh knuckles on the coonter, waitin.

"Where is it?" she shouts. "What have you done with it? Did you sell it?"

"Whit are ye lookin fir, Senga?" Eh says, ken, and acts the daft lassie.

"You know fine well what I'm looking for. The dress! The Vera Vanstone dress that I was going to wear to my grandson's Christening in the Woodlands."

Eh slides aff the stool and says, "Oh dae ye mean the frock aff yir special rail at the back, the ane wi the covered buttons and the dangly things hingin doon the front?"

"Yes!" she says, and her ehs close again and the chin goes up!

"Actually, Senga, eh gave it awa."

"You what! You gave it away!" she shrieks.

"Well yi see," eh tells her, "this wummin came inta the shop at dennertime and wis looking for frocks. Particular frocks she asked for. She described the frocks, and eh got ti thinkin, mibbee it's they anes in the back, especially when the wummin said they were labelled and you said they were quality. We could be maakin serious money here for Charity First! So eh took the wummin through ti the back and showed her the rail."

"That's them! That's them! My sister's dresses!" the wifie shouted.

Well, Senga's fais wis a picture. She wis bilin.

"And you gave them away?" If looks could kill, eh'd be daed!

"See the thing wis, Senga," eh says, "this wifie's sister had dehd

CHARITY FIRST

a few weeks back in the Shady Pines nursin home alang the road there, and her man had handed in her claes ti the shop, and of coorse the wifie didna ken this, and had waanted ti hae some o her sister's claes as a wee keepsake."

"And you gave her the dress! How could you possibly know it belonged to her?"she says. "You've been well and truly had, Agnes, and done me out of my designer staff purchase to which I was entitled."

Eh sidled back ti the coonter and once eh wis firmly perched on the stool, eh said, "No, YOU'VE got it a rang, Senga, it wis definitely her sister's frocks. The nursing home stitched her name inta her claes! It wis her sister's name that wis on the label –Vera Vanstone!"

Well! Her fais wis a pitcher. Senga grabs her bag and tells me ti lock the shop up on the wy oot!

Eh pissed mesel ah the wy hame on the bus. Wait till eh tell Pat and Izzie this ane, eh thought. Oh! Before eh forgit, eh left twa pound on the coonter for the Jaeger Jeckit – minus the twenty per cent staff discount of course!

BE CAREFUL WHAT YOU WISH FOR

June Cadden

Daphne could not say that she was entirely happy with her lot. She should have been. After all, she had married well but there was always that glint in her eyes – the one that made almost everyone she met feel inferior. It was a knack she had nurtured and even perfected over the years – compensation perhaps for the lack of the double-barrelled surname that she had always thought would one day be hers. Mrs Hamilton-Smythe had had other ideas for her beloved boy and Daphne did not figure in any of the imagined future plans for him.

Bernard Lefèvre, on the other hand, was more open to Daphne's charms. In those days she would hang on his every word and even laugh at his lame jokes. Well, she had to. She'd been his secretary.

On their marriage Daphne threw herself into becoming the Mrs Professor that she had worked so hard to become. Coffee mornings with the other Mrs Professors were de rigueur. She didn't want to invite them to the house of course, not even Cyril's closest colleague, Eugene, and his mousey little wife, Elizabeth. Oh no, she didn't want them snooping around and gossiping behind her back. The anonymity of the golf club suited her to a tee.

With the birth of Cyril her life changed yet again. Oh yes, Cyril was to eclipse even his illustrious father. Now wouldn't that be something – two professors in the same family? He would get his chair, she mused, have a syndrome that he had discovered named after him and on the way make a marvellous marriage. She wouldn't interfere, well, not more than was good for Cyril.

What had not figured on Daphne's radar was the fact that Cyril turned out to be a serial marrier. Like it or not, it became obvious that the first marriage was going to fail. She wasn't surprised and she wasn't that upset either. Her equilibrium quickly returned when Cyril turned up one day with Cynthia Burnett-McLeod. Daphne warmed to her immediately. It could be said that the arrogance of one woman matched

BE CAREFUL WHAT YOU WISH FOR

that of the other and Cynthia had Cyril completely under her spell.

After a while, however, Daphne noticed that Cyril was growing tired of being required to say: "Yes, my dear, no, my dear, whatever you wish, my dear" and when Cynthia became prone to one cold after the next, that was the last straw. Cyril had no bedside manner, his mother knew that, and he was a hypochondriac to boot. Cyril didn't do illness and he didn't do marriage to Cynthia either.

Daphne, of course, now had hopes that her son would come back to live with her and Bernard. She had said as much to her husband who just buried his nose even further into his newspaper.

One day when she came back in from one of the golf club coffee mornings Bernard announced to her that Cyril had rung. He told her that he was visiting at the week-end with Cassie.

"Cassie, Cassie who?"

"Apparently she's engaged to him, so I suppose that you'd call her his fiancée, dearest," Bernard replied.

"Don't you 'dearest' me! My nerves are still in shock from the last one."

"Yes, dearest," Bernard muttered, and with that he was back to his crossword.

The visit was not a success. It was never going to be, right from the moment when her prospective daughter-in-law addressed her as 'Mrs The Fever'. Through clenched teeth Daphne had repeated: 'Le-fev-rre' but Cassie merely smiled a wider smile which was only matched by the one Bernard was also sporting.

Cyril, oblivious to most things – he was an academic after all – seemed very happy with how things had gone and even said to his mother before they left: "Cassie's made a real effort today, ma. She's a one-off isn't she, a real ray of sunshine?"

Those were not the words that Daphne herself would have chosen to describe the woman – tornado perhaps but not ray of sunshine. Perhaps Cyril had been referring to the orange and pink fluffy number that passed for the top Cassie had chosen to wear that day. Two sizes too small, if you ask me, was what Daphne thought and how low-cut for someone with her cleavage. It didn't seem to bother Bernard, quite the opposite, and Daphne could have sworn that he had dropped his newspaper on purpose just so that Cassie would bend down in front of him and pick it up. Daphne couldn't decide which had been worse, the top or the pencil-thin short skirt that accompanied it. 1960's seaside postcard came to mind.

She had wanted to warn her beloved son off marrying someone she considered to be totally unsuitable but in the end didn't. She could not face the thought of living in that barn of a house with no visits from Cyril. There was always the possibility, she thought, that Cassie might decide to let him come on his own and then she could pretend that nothing had changed.

After they left Daphne took to her bed and stayed there for most of the following day. The same question kept going through her mind: how could he, how could he do this to me? There was no room in her mind for wondering whether he had, in fact, found true happiness at last.

Cyril and Cassie did get married. It was a register office job. Just Bernard, Cassie's foster parents and the happy couple were present. There was not going to be a photo in the local rag so what was the point of an expensive new dress and hat? In the end Daphne settled for an M&S outfit. The next day she unpicked a seam in the dress, took it back, and got a refund. She didn't want the memory of what she had considered a back-street wedding lingering on in her mind.

Cassie came over to her after the ceremony, flaunting her platinum wedding ring which sat next to an equally expensive engagement ring – all sapphires and diamonds.

"So, I'll be calling you 'mum' from now on, shan't I?" she said.

Daphne's look said it all.

Future visits would have been strained had it not been for the fact that Cassie busied herself with making Bernard laugh, allowing Daphne to have Cyril all to herself. She often wondered what plans Cassie and Bernard were hatching as they would fall silent when she entered the room and then burst out laughing when they thought that she was out of earshot. She had questioned Bernard about this and told him that their behaviour oppressed her.

"Don't you mean 'obsessed', dearest?" Bernard remarked wryly.

She could not work out why Bernard had taken to Cassie so well but he told her it was because Cassie didn't play-act, and that what you saw was what you got. He added that he felt that she deserved all the love and happiness that might come her way after having been put into care at such an early age.

BE CAREFUL WHAT YOU WISH FOR

Two years later Bernard was dead. Cassie was heart-broken, Cyril confused and Daphne resigned. After the funeral there was the reading of the will. Daphne knew that everything would come to her; it was just a question of when. The solicitor then announced that Bernard had left Cassie all his shares in the Hong Kong and Shanghai Bank. Daphne felt quite faint and asked for a glass of water.

"Oh, he'll have left you shares as well, ma," said Cyril. "That's what he was like – thoughtful."

Bernard had indeed left his wife shares – in a not so well-known bank called Lehman Brothers.

Cyril and Cassie dropped Daphne off at 'the barn', as Cassie liked to call it, in Camphill Road. She didn't ask them in for a drink.

After a few years Daphne began to wonder whether Cyril would ever announce that Cassie was pregnant. It wasn't that she particularly liked children or even hankered to be a grandmother. It was just that everyone in the coffee circle had photos to pass round and she felt peeved that she couldn't join in. Then came the day that Cyril rang.

"Ma, I've got something that I need to tell you. Any chance of a wee drinkie in the next few days?"

Daphne, feeling that she would soon have photos of her own, was all too pleased to agree. So Cyril arrived, a bit agitated she felt, but then that was only to be expected with him fast approaching fifty. He sat down, drink in hand, nervous, cleared his throat and said: "I'm coming out."

"Where?" asked Daphne. "Anywhere nice?"

"No, ma, you don't understand. I've decided I can't go on like this. It was pa's death that decided me. He said to Cassie that he was so pleased that she had finally found someone to love her for what she is. Well, it got me thinking. I realised that that was what I wanted too."

"Well, that's music to my ears. You've finally realised that that woman is not the one for you."

"What woman? Oh, no I realised that years ago."

"So, why did you marry her?"

"Well, she made me laugh."

"So, tell me son, who's the lucky girl?" She knew him well enough to realise that he couldn't face life on his own.

"Ma, you're not taking this in, are you? There is no lucky girl.

Cassie and I have parted amicably. She was upset but said that she understood. No, ma, I'm marrying Perry, well sort of."

"And does she work with you?"

"Perry is short for Peregrine. Ma, I'm gay. So when can I bring him to meet you?"

Oh dear, this was worse than the reading of the will. No grandchildren then, Daphne brightened momentarily – and no Cassie anymore either. That was a silver lining but then Perry was the cloud within it now. Perry, Perry... What was wrong with Cyril? Was this a joke?

It wasn't a joke. The 'wedding' was nothing like she had ever experienced and the last straw was when one of the more exotic guests complimented her on her cross-dressing.

Her shares proved worthless but she sold the barn and left the country. The surrogate family was more than she could bear. Cyril, it seemed, had at last found true love and was in his element being a house husband, or was that wife, Daphne wasn't sure. He was, she had to admit a good cook. Well, he'd had enough women to be able to learn from.

Daphne couldn't bring herself to ring Cyril to tell him that she was going far away. She left a letter with the solicitor but there was no address to be seen anywhere in it.

THE BEAUTIFUL HYPOTHESIS

Roddie McKenzie

Dr Eugene Travers MBChB, MD stroked his smooth, cologne-scented chin with one hand while the other tentatively held the graph up to the watery March light. The sunlight drew a pale glow from his crisp white lab coat and the nascent waves of grey hair flowing back from his temples. The paper was still soft and damp – like a used tissue – the data being hot off the inkjet printer. His pale blue eyes darted back and forth as he followed the red and black curves. The chin stroking slowed and stopped as the thin trace of a smile crossed his lips.

Ye-esss. The protective effect of the antisera was going up with the applied dose. It confirmed the initial experiment. The rate of chin stroking increased gradually. This was a great antidote to his Monday blues.

"So what do you think, Eugene? Looks pretty cool, eh?" Kelly-Ann, his PhD student, was leaning her elbows on the bench, her lab coat open as her elfin face swung up to meet his.

His deliberations interrupted, Eugene winced at the contemporary salutation and looked down, momentarily docking with Kelly-Ann's eyes. Doing an ocular body swerve around her cleavage, he misjudged it and ended up addressing the glass ranks of chemical solutions on the shelf above her head.

To claw back the initiative, he rolled out the jargon and stifled his leaping enthusiasm. "Yes, it is clearly an interesting development, but could equally represent a random event."

"But I *have* done it three times now and got the same result. Looks pretty wicked to me." Kelly-Ann bounced up off her elbow and rammed her hands into the hip pockets of her lab coat. The lapels stuck up like the barbs on razor wires.

"*Wicked*?" Eugene harumphed. "That is not a term that will command much respect at the British Skin Cancer Society meeting; you really must be more specific."

Kelly-Ann's hands were out of her lab coat and her red hair

flicked back at the speed of petrol igniting. Her forehead furrowed and the pout could only be milliseconds away.

"Well, I thought that you'd be pleased, but I will set it up again."

As Kelly-Ann turned away her arms began that petulant swing. Why did she have to be so damned bolshie? Then he remembered he had had twenty-two years of the opposite extreme with Elizabeth and look how that ended up. Eugene relented.

"Kelly-Ann, I'm… maybe… I'm not sharing your joy enough. I appreciate that you have put a lot into this." The words they had taught him on the supervisors' refresher course were unfamiliar, sickly-sweet in his mouth. She stopped the arm swinging.

"Look, think on more results, better statistics. Firm this up and it could be 'news off the press'. It's that type of opportunity that opens doors; you know when I was…"

"Well they looked good enough to me but you're the man, Boss."

Why was she so obstructive! With a flick he released the damp printout over the bench where it dived like a stalled airliner. His chest swelled as he pulled his shoulders back.

"In any case, I want to see your talk, including another repeat of the antibody titration on Thursday in seminar room B at 2 pm."

She looked at him, her lips moved, but silently, and her eyes fell as she turned away.

As Kelly-Ann marched the red dot of the laser pointer through the data, Eugene sank back in his seat in the semi-darkened seminar room full of admiration. Her data was elegantly presented. She had learned well from him but there was something more, a natural ease with which she described the highlights of the results, while not shying away from the shortcomings inevitable in any experiment. He found his gaze drawn to her form, a dark rolling silhouette against the bright primary colours displayed on the slide screen. On one level he despised these unprofessional thoughts, but on another they seemed to provide something sweet to ruminate on and it was a long while since that had been the case. Coming back to business, Eugene was now convinced that – unconventional as she was – she had potential, possibly greater even than Hassan, who had published six papers under his guidance.

During his turmoil, Kelly-Ann had talked breezily through the final slide, the acknowledgements. She stopped talking and turned to him. It took him a moment to come around and the silence gaped before he broke into applause.

"Superb, Kelly-Ann: a great talk. You have come on so much since the last section seminars. You handled the data masterfully, and you are so much more at ease. How was it for you?"

Kelly-Ann looked incredulous before finding his meaning. "Yeah, I thought it was cool. I felt okay, not too rushed, not too slow… Yeah! It rocked!"

"Yes… indeed, it's the best delivery from you that I have heard. You know, I think that the Sensation Science Cafe programme would be a great place to start showcasing this exciting piece of work. I've taken the liberty of putting you on the programme for next Friday evening."

The colour drained from her face.

"Eugene, I've got plans. It's our band's three year anniversary gig, a lot of people are expecting to see us."

He felt the heat flash over his cheeks. "Do you want to make a career out of science or not? These opportunities don't come along all the time you know. A researcher has to be seen and you never seem to make any of the summer meetings."

As she started to speak he brought the hammer down. "As your supervisor, I expect you to present. If you don't make an apearance, I *will* be bringing this up with your supervisors' committee. The subject is closed."

Kelly-Ann wrenched her pen drive from the computer and sensing the mood, Travers picked up his papers and quickly left, choosing not to acknowledge the stabbing middle finger silhouetted on the screen in his peripheral vision. He was doing it for her own good. She would thank him.

The following week Eugene enjoyed a cool détente with Kelly-Ann. Though she seemed a bit agitated on Thursday, she kept up with her lab work, even if, when he passed her office, he was aware of the omnipresent electric guitar case by her desk. On Friday morning he had discussed the matter at one of his regular appointments with Sylvia Revey, the staff counsellor, whom he had been seeing since Elizabeth left. Eugene felt the session had gone well. He discussed all his students with her, but Kelly-Ann in particular.

As he strolled along the Perth road on Friday, en route to Sensation, he passed the blind man who so often seemed to walk this way. Not to be able to see things clearly… it was a thought that made Eugene shudder and he found himself side-stepping the man as he replayed the highlights of his conversation with Sylvia.

"I'm sorry to interrupt Eugene but I'm a little confused. You have voiced concern about her *origin*s, for want of a better word, before. I understand that she came into the degree programme through an HND route. Are you saying that because of this she does not make the grade? I am afraid I don't see the relevance. The fact is that she *is* in a PhD programme now."

"Well… I just wish she would be more co-operative, more collegiate. I mean, she insists on continuing to play in her group or 'band' as she calls it. When I was in her position, I leapt at every chance to get my work in the public view. Science is not an easy mistress. Your efforts have to be concentrated. It takes dedication – single-minded sacrifice for the greater good."

"And *you* do not think that Kelly-Ann is up for that?"

"She obviously made the grade, but her family has no academic background; I don't think that she realises what this work involves."

"So you say the work needs the sacrifice, the merciless focus…"

"Indeed, that was what *I* had to do."

"I see."

He hoped now that Sylvia Revey would share his reservations about Kelly-Ann.

When Eugene arrived at Sensation, the crowd were already filling the seats. A curious mixture he thought. There were two distinct tribes – those of the slacks and fleece and those of the indie tattered jeans and plaid shirts. The slide screen was huge above the stage but he did not understand the presence of the instruments and drums. Perhaps there was entertainment later in the evening.

Professor Sir James Hamilton, the famous cancer biologist, was there with a few of the great and the good of the Wellcome Building. Eugene loitered on the periphery of their circle and was eventually invited to join the conversation. Yes, one of his students *was* presenting this evening and there *did* seem to be an unusually large turnout. They took their seats as the first talk was announced.

Kelly-Ann took the stage and to Eugene's horror, a ragged band of musicians shuffled into position to the spacy sounds of guitar tuning.

THE BEAUTIFUL HYPOTHESIS

His head spun and a sickness filled the pit of his stomach. Kelly Ann plucked the mic from its stand and waved to the crowd, turning slowly in a semi-circle to face them all in turn. This was outrageous! Had she no respect? The people he had invited…He must stop this travesty; he rose to his feet, calves trembling, as he hunched in the cramped row.

"Good evening, folks, and welcome to Science Sessions at Sensation! Tonight, in a break from the usual format, I'm going to tell you about the hot-from-the-bench-developments in skin cancer research. I'll be assisted in this multi-media presentation by…" Kelly-Ann rolled her wrist out and indicated, "from Dundee, *The Fabulous Coomassie Blues Band"*. A burst of applause and unacademic foot stamping broke out from the indie tribe, to the alarm of the ranked fleeces. She clicked the handset. Eugene's courage deserted him and he sat down.

The room darkened and projected on a big screen above the stage, a benevolent sun rose as the band softly picked out the tune of *Here comes the sun*. Kelly-Ann changed the slides and explained about ultraviolet radiation before that song faded and a giant schematic coloured image of a section of skin rose like a wall thanks to Powerpoint animation. The band switched to the cranked bass line of The Stranglers' *Skin Deep* instrumental as Kelly-Ann made the scientific points, but with their brief intonation of the choruses when she took a break. Eugene could not look at the once familiar, friendly graphs. This time both camps clapped and cheered. Sir James looked at Eugene askance.

The forty-five minutes flew in and for the finale a great red angry sun writhed in video, throwing up arcs of flame. Kelly-Ann slung on her red Telecaster and hit the first chords of the *The Ultraviolet Blues*. As the beat picked up to a rapid stride she flailed out the chords, her hair tossed, necklace bounced and swung and her rolled up shirt exposed the Celtic knot tattooed on her upper arm. And the words poured out in hot rush:

> *Going to be some changes round here,*
> *Now the ozone`s gone.*
> *No more March break way down South*
> *No more skinny dipping in the lake,*
> *The weenie's a terrible thing to bake*
> *Sun block 1000 is the latest scam –*
> *Score you a deal for £100 a gram*

She mumbled the last line surreptiously. Later as the electric climax rolled away to fade out, the crowd rose together and clapped and cheered. Kelly-Ann was bowing and smiling to the crowd, to the band, but Travers refused to catch her eye as the twisting in his stomach tightened his nerves. He was going to be sick. As his head flailed around Sir James slapped his shoulder, his face creased with laugher.

"This is the best talk I've been at in years! This is just what science needs to get to the public!"

Eugene nodded like a puppet as he rose and hurried to the exit.

Eugene was low, foot achingly low, as Sylvia Revey plied him gently with questions. He was confused; it wasn't jealousy of the headlines that Kelly-Ann had garnered in *The Courier: Biggest turnout at Sensation breaks the stuffy perception of scientists.*

It didn't even seem to be the fact that Kelly-Ann had requested a change in research schools. He realised that it wasn't going to work between them. It was the irreverence of it all.

"Eugene, I know you take your work very seriously, the hours you put in..."

"Well, you've got to – what is it they say? Pay your dues?"

"You have sacrificed so much and – from what you have said – sacrificed Elizabeth as well?"

He found the words too painful. After some moments he nodded.

"And if someone did not take science *seriously*?"

"Well it would be demeaning. Science is a serious subject."

"I see. How about Professor Brian Cox? He clearly is a competent scientist but he has a family, appears on TV and, indeed, once played in a band."

He blustered. "Well, I can't say... I don't know the man."

"I'm wondering whether an affront to 'science', is actually an affront to *your* values, Eugene? Perhaps what Kelly-Ann did was an affront to the way that you have chosen to live your life?"

"All I was trying to do was give her a hand up. God knows no-one ever did it for me. And all this band nonsense flies in the face of all *my* efforts! She could have been someone. She was immature, bolshie, but perhaps... like the daughter... I..."

He stopped, flustered and blushing, noticing he was perched on the edge of his chair, his hands up, fingers stabbing the air.

THE BEAUTIFUL HYPOTHESIS

"She probably will be somebody. But she must live her life, Eugene, and you can't live yours vicariously."

He melted back in the chair as the anger blew over leaving a chilling epiphany.

After a few moments she said, "Eugene, I'm afraid our time is up. I'm sorry I should have warned you about the time sooner. Please, feel free to sit for a few minutes, take your time."

Eugene closed the door of Sylvia's office and walked along the empty, after-hours corridor of the Counselling Department. He paused at the stair head window.

On the Fife hills, the snow had gone now, as quickly and as unnoticed as the years – his wasted years, far behind. The warm tears on his cheek shocked him into recognising the contrasting glacial cold and polar emptiness in his heart.

IT FEELS LIKE YEARS

Chris Smith

Each afternoon, Colin Fisher tapped his way down the Perth Road and swung the big loop past the station to land up at the Discovery. Each afternoon, after the home help had been or the meals on wheels; a different time, but each afternoon in the good weather. He didn't do rain, snow or sleet. His flat cap was pulled down to secure it against any wind, any cheeky gust which might threaten his dignity. A donkey jacket buttoned from top to bottom. A penguin with a white cane tap tapping, swaying, rolling along.

At the Discovery, he sat outside the dock. He just sat. Thirty minutes. He sat. The sea gulls bristled but stayed aloof. If it was cold, he'd thrust his hands deep into his pockets, the cane hooked under one armpit across his body. Slouched back, he seemed to mock the gulls, inviting a confrontation. That never happened. The cane, a stick with which to beat them.

He was listening. He was training himself to hear. The first weeks, it was just the Tay, just the river. Then in days, the ebb, the flow, the calm of the smooth water flowing to Perth, the chop as it returned against a breeze. The landscape in his ears broadened. The birds squawked. They came closer as gulls. The harmonics under their wings as they hovered and jerked in the same breeze as the chop.

The coach in the car park with the flock of noisy children. Young, still shrill children. Not the mumbling deep rumbles of the boys who skateboarded just before the traffic that masked the station that the city stood behind. He imagined.

It was more than near or far, left or right. Sometimes he felt he squeezed the sounds in the air to dribble a meaning. That motorbike was coming from the west along Riverside Drive. More than the legal limit and there was a suggestion of misfiring. The Olympia car parking. The woman talking to a small child, words indistinct but articulate and angry. The boot of the car opened, a push chair's wheels jangled to the

IT FEELS LIKE YEARS

pavement as the chair snapped into shape. Flustered. Closer to hand, a couple cooing about the feeding habits of seagulls.

He was learning to put a distance between here, now, and then. Too late. The last day he woke with some sight. That morning he got up and swatted the air. His wife was burning the toast again. This time, it was strangely odourless. He stumbled out of the bedroom and bumped into furniture as he struggled to open the living room window. The Derby Road multi sixteen floors up and the view was a vista to all the world and the rest of Fife. But now it was all swirling mist, haar and grey indistinct and it still swirled as much as the wind howled around the window. His wife's voice from outside the grey. "Whatever is the matter, Colin?"

The days that followed he heard doctors peer into his eyes. He got used to being led into different rooms at Ninewells Hospital.

"Good afternoon, Mr… um… Fisher. How are you? Yes. Come on in, Mrs Fisher, you can join us. Now, let's just check these notes. Right, has he been taking the drops? Have you noticed any changes?"

Two sighted people having a conversation. Kind but sighted. There was nothing to be done. It had been too late. He should have said something sooner.

Their home became his prison. He couldn't get on with the stairs, the intermittent lifts. He couldn't get on with a dog. He couldn't sit alone in front of a view.

They moved. Ground floor maisonette, around the corner. It was the last thing she did for him. The first months were bruised shins, walking into walls they didn't have, and her dry cough.

It was a Senior Service cough. It was a Ninewells again, cough. He heard the hacking smallness as she passed.

He was trying to remember. But everything dissolved. Her face was there but the colour of her eyes weren't. 985 steps from the fish bar at the bottom of Perth Road to Mennies but how many years? He buried her in 1998 but couldn't remember the last time they kissed as man and wife. In quiet moments, he wanted to.

But today, he was getting fed up and tired. Holding back thirteen years was head work. Let's go for a pint. Sit in the peace and quiet. Turn off these thoughts. Stop the nonsense.

The Discovery was creaking behind him. If you pulled the rub of wood to wood close and dissected it and put your head right into the middle of it, the dowels carried the smallest voices of the shipwrights talking across themselves as they hammered in the threads of notes. Sometimes, he felt their vibration and could see them leaning across the bow observing him. Over the years, it became more distinct and very soon he would be able to turn, look over his shoulder, and say 'hello'. Out loud.

Right. Enough. Let's go for that pint. Now. And a wee treat. A stop in the Co-op chemist. That lassie with the smell of old fashioned bath salts and cheery smile.

He got himself to his feet, pulled his jacket down, back and front. He paused and turned to face towards the pedestrian crossing, like a missile locking on its target. And he was off.

The traffic was getting busy. The station seemed noisy enough for four o'clock. An hour to Eddie Mair. The sun was warm for May. That bus was a stinky diesel. There used to be a Tele kiosk on the Overgate corner. When did that go?

Chips. She always liked a single fish. Yes. She did. Well done. Well remembered. A single fish.

He walked up past the university and felt the students walk around him as they passed. At about ten feet, he could still hear the footsteps coming right at him and the little jink in pressure when they realised and manoeuvred. He always noted their hesitancy .

Then the home stretch, the wee shops. Wee Jeanie who cut the hair. Jamie's lad who worked for Tom Farmer across the road. Two coffee places with the roast aroma. Nigel the florist. The Royal Bank. And Mennies, at last.

A fair thirst. Three steps in. Turn right, if no one was standing in front of you; then order. Those you knew said, "Hello Colin". The miseries let you guess. Pint in front, touch gently, in hand. Take a sip to allow the carrying of said pint.

Back the way into the room with no tele. Used to be the snug in the olden days.

In the room on his own, he placed his drink in front of him on the table. Colin took off his cap, placed it on one knee and ran his hand through this hair. He folded the cane and put it in his jacket pocket.

He felt someone slide into the chair opposite him across the table. He felt sure he was alone. The room had been flat, dead and empty when he came in.

"A'right grand-da. Anyone sittin' here?"

Thin vowel voice. Liverpool-ish. Oh no, a scouser. A comedian.

"No, son. You're fine." He was definitely close and opposite. Four feet. But no glass. Sandalwood or rosewater; a transparent essence in the air.

"I know this is gonna sound soft, mister. And, I don't want to bother you like. But, is this Dundee?"

He sounded sincere. Probably just a bit stupid.

"As far as I can tell. This is Dundee."

"It's only, I came here a long time ago. I think it was a couple times, with ma pals. And what with, I've been travelling and stuff and we've not seen each other. I just wondered why I pitched up here." There was a creak as his weight shifted in the chair.

"Interrupting good drinking time."

"Sorry mister, I didn't notice anyone having a good time. Just a grumpy old git scaring seagulls on his own like some kinda nutter. Then stompin' off to the boozer like a diddy." His tone was cheeky.

"There's no need for that tone, especially…"

"As I hardly know you. Yeah. Shockin. Aye shockin. 'How does he know what I was going to say? Why does he need to finish my sentences for me? How does he know my name? Colin.' To be honest, I don't know either. It's been one of those days." He sounded deflated, weary.

"I just stopped for a drink on my way home for my tea."

"And you missed that girl at the chemist."

"And I missed the wee lassie and I am just not in the mood for a blether or pleasant chat with a stranger to lighten their load. To make them feel welcome. And you can piss off and all. And if I look sullen then it's because I am grumpy." Colin took a sip for effect and held his palm up towards the man; holding the ground. "This is my pub, my pint, and my time."

"Ta-da. That was some speech. You could have been some song writer you." He sang back, " This is my pub, going to the end of the line. This is my pint… all in the key of G , eh Colin?"

Colin sat up, stung. There was taking the rise and then there was taking liberties. He reached into his pocket for his cane.

"Don't you stir yourself, Colin. I'll go. You are not the only person in this picture. Take care. Nice talking to you. "

Chris Smith

After the man left, Colin sat there in a silence he didn't like. He went home to a silence he didn't like, an Eddie Mair he didn't like and some crisp cheese on toast he didn't like.

The next morning, it rained in that cold way May has to persuade you that summer will follow soon. There was the compensation of a new John Grisham audio book in the midday post. The following day was bright and dry. The Discovery was a joy and the shipwrights were nearly there. Colin would have sworn a Stagecoach bus bound for Fife braked sharply as it approached the roundabout at the far end of the Tay Bridge. He was on his game and it was that kind of a day.

"Diddy," he snorted.

In the snug on his own, he placed his drink in front of him on the table. He took off his cap, placed it on one knee and ran his hand through this hair. He folded the cane and put it in his jacket pocket. There was a tremor in the air. He sensed the sandalwood before he heard the light tread and scrape of the pub chair as it eased back.

"A'right grand-da . Anyone sittin' here?"

"Oh. It's you."

The space between them was comfortable. Colin felt smiled at.

"Listen. About the other day. It's not that I am particularly unfriendly or whatever…"

"'…it's just I've a lot on my mind.' Yeah Colin, I understand. I could have said that myself. I don't understand this bodhisattva thing. How do I end up in a pub with a guy I have never met?"

"What's there to understand? You're young; you go in pubs, you annoy people. Just grow up."

"Easy for you to say. I am carrying people, things, stuff and karma. I am trying, like, to work it out but it's so tough. If it was just religion, it would be easy. If I'm here for a point then you're here for a point."

It all sounded too wishy-washy. Thought for the day pap. The lad was patronising him or trying to.

"Son. It's easy. In the pub, it's every man for himself or maybe, by himself. Just you remember that."

There was a long pause.

"Colin, you are some guy. Drowning out the world. You know, the boat thing…"

IT FEELS LIKE YEARS

"You know nothing. When you've had a life, you can tell me something. You can lecture me. I had it all. I lost everything. Just everything. You don't have the first idea what it is like to lose your sight."

"Was that the hardest thing to lose?" The voice was soft and close.

He could see her face very clearly. Her eyes were hazel and she was smiling. All so clear.

"Yes. It was."

He got up and pushed the table away as he pulled his jacket down, back and front. He wanted to act dignified. No one spoke to him like that. No one could judge him, his pain, his suffering. There were 335 reluctant steps to his front door. He counted them that evening.

The next day, the first day of June was actually hot and full of warm pavements and faces. After his lunch was delivered, Colin wondered about heading out but hesitated. He couldn't face it.

It was nearly a week before Colin found himself listening to the Discovery again. He seemed rusty and unsettled. He listened listlessly and his concentration was all over the place. The soup of sound tired him. Waves slapped against the river bank steps, a plane impossibly blended with a train and the wind moaned words reversed. He struggled to make any sense of it.

Time to get away. Stop for a drink but somewhere different. It had to be done.

The bar was new, different because it was difficult. He stood there. It sounded big and empty except at the edges. The central noise was muzak. The glass was wet, hints of lemon washing up liquid and it was too gassy. Colin sighed.

He put his pint down. He stood up, pulled his jacket down, back and front. He smiled; this was the wrong bar. He didn't have a point here.

GUS 'N' US

David Francis

We call him Gus, short for Gallus, for that's what he is. He always has that 'wha dare meddle wi me?' look to him. He stands about two feet high, gey spindly legs but he could take your finger off with one bite. He could have your face off, if you upset him.

I should've said no when she offered him to me, if offered is the right word. Margaret – a working girl, if you know what I mean. Margaret and I we'd just, well… completed a transaction, if you know what I mean. And we're just lying there, sharing a fag and having a wee blether when there's this almighty crash from her kitchen and a banging and a screeching. "What the hell is that?!" I'm out the bed like a shot from a gun. She's sticking her head under the covers. "Oh no!"

So I'm trying to open the kitchen door and it's stuck and there's still this banging and screeching. And then a boy's shouting from out in the close, "Going to shut that fucking racket up!?" And I'm shouting, "It's no me!" And she's still going, "Oh no, oh no." And I'm pushing at the door and pushing and pushing and there's something behind it. And then the door gives and I go my length into a pile of pots and pans and couped chairs. So I'm flat on my face on the deck in the scud in a heap of kitchen utensils and furniture and there's a bottle of Mazola on its side on the bunker and it's dripping all over the floor.

And I look up and there it is – stupid big thing just sitting on the top of the wall units. "How in the name of God did that get in here?" And then she's at the kitchen door wrapped up in her downie. "I brought him in." "You what?" And I'm trying to stand up and I'm sliding all over with the oil on the floor and my bits are all waving about and she starts laughing. So I just slide down and sit with my back to the bunker, where I can keep an eye on the thing where it is, hunched between the top of the units and the ceiling, giving me that badass look.

"He's done that before but maybe not quite so spectacularly. He gets on top of the kitchen chairs but he's no steady enough on them and they coup over and he gets a fright and he jumps up onto the top of the units where all the pans are... or were."

"Wait a minute, wait a minute, I'm still wanting to know how he got here."

"I told you, I brought him in."

"Why did you do that?"

"I felt sorry for him."

"Sorry for him?"

"Aye, he'd been hanging about out on the back green for days, all gawky like, never went anywhere, kept getting dive bombed by crows. He found his way up to my window one day and I thought he looked a bit peely wally."

"Peely wally?"

"Aye, ken, a wee bit pasty."

"A wee bit pasty? "

"Aye."

"Did it not occur to you that the delicate pale hue of his features was entirely as nature intended? – seen as how he *is* a bloody seagull! He's just not got it in him to look tanned and fit. And what do you mean he's done it before?"

"Well, he has. He doesn't like it when I have to shut him in here, ken, when I've got a customer, like. He got out one time when a guy was using the loo. Come up behind him and pecked his arse. The guy near had a heart attack. Called me for everything under the sun."

"Guess he'll no be a returning customer then."

"No, probably not. And, you see, that's the problem, he's a bit of a liability."

"Aye, I can see how he might be."

"You wouldn't like to do me a big favour and take him, would you?"

"And what am I going to do with him?"

"Well you stay on your own and he'd be good company."

"Good company? Listen, I'm quite capable of wrecking my own kitchen just making my dinner, I don't need any help, and I certainly don't need my bum nipping while I'm having a waz. And talking of which, where does he, you know... relieve himself?"

"Oh, we had a few accidents at the start but he's quite good now. I shooed him out onto the windowsill and he seems to have got the idea. He taps on the window when he needs to go."

"So how do you not just leave him there outside and maybe he'll fly away."

"No he'll no do that. He taps on the window to get back in and if you don't let him he just taps harder and harder. One time I thought he was going to put the whole window in."

"Aye, he knows a cushy number when he sees one. I suppose you feed him and all?"

"Aye."

"What do you feed him on?"

"He likes a fish supper. And on a Sunday I give him a mince roll."

"He's definitely a Dundee seagull then."

"Go on, you've got to help me, I really quite like him but he's going to put me out of business."

"Well that's maybe no a bad thing. A lovely girl like you shouldn't have to do what you do."

"Well I don't really have much choice. It's that or starve. And don't you get on your high horse, pal, because you come round here, don't you?"

"Yeh, but I really like you. It's no like you're a stranger."

"Do you?"

"Do I what?"

"Really like me?"

"Aye, you know I do."

"No I don't, you never said."

"Well I do. That's why I always like to stay for a wee smoke and a chat."

"Aye, you always do and I like that too. It's no like you're a stranger."

"No."

"If you really like me, will you do me a favour?"

"You mean take him?"

"Aye, go on. You told me you like watching all those animal programmes on the telly."

"Aye, but that's all about the jungle and lions and tigers and stuff. It's no about Dundee and seagulls and I'm no David Attenborough. How would we get him down?"

"Well he seems a wee bit calmer now so we might get him down with a fish supper."

"Why don't we push the boat out and get him scampi?"

"Get through by and get yourself dressed and then away to the chipper."

"And then what?"

"Well I don't want him causing any more mayhem in here so we can lure him down to the end of the close and you can hide at the bottom of the stairs and get a hold of him down there."

"Then what?"

"I've got a laundry bag. You can pop him in there and take him round to your place. It's not far."

"You're joking. Look at the size of the bugger."

"It's a big bag."

"You don't imagine for one moment he's going to come quietly do you? 'Here you are, nice birdie, just hop in here.' And why would I take him round to my place? Why can't we just get him away from here and then release him back into the wild?"

"See, there, you've got all the lingo – I knew you'd have learned something from all those nature programmes."

"Well, why don't I just do that? All that matters is that he's out of here."

"You can't just throw him out. It's dark out there and the crows'll duff him up. Besides he's used to his creature comforts now. I'd be happier if he went to a good home."

"A good home? It's no like he's a pet, like a cat or a dog or something."

"Aye he is. It's like having a budgie – just bigger."

"You're as daft as he is. All right, all right, I'll take him round to my place for a day or two but then he's getting repatriated, back to the wild."

So, twenty minutes later I'm walking backwards down the stair of her close laying a trail of chips and this guy comes out his door and says, "What are you doing?" And I says, "I'm trying to catch a seagull." And he says, "Cheeky bastard!" and slams his door.

Anyway, once the trail was laid and the laundry bag was got out – and she was right, it was huge, it was also day-glo pink – once we were ready, we went back into the kitchen with a bit of the fish to tempt the big bugger down. She threw the fish from the kitchen door over onto the bunker with what, I have to say, was a pretty good throw for a lassie and straight away the big fella jumped down to get it. Only he's that desperate to get it and he's that clumsy that he lands on the Mazola bottle where it's all slippy and the feet go from under him and he dunts his head on the side of the bunker and knocks himself clean out.

"Oh ya beauty!"

"Oh no! How can you say that?! Look, he's hurt himself. He's banged his head!"

"Yeh, OK, I know, I know, it's a shame but it's not like there's a lot in there to get damaged and now we can get him in the bag without a wrestling match."

Aye, so it was a spot of luck but I don't know if you've ever tried to put a fully grown herring gull into a laundry bag, even quite a big pink laundry bag, but let me tell you, it isn't easy. We managed to get him folded up and we were as gentle as we could be – her because she was, as she kept telling him, "So sorry" and me because I didn't want the bugger waking up and then me having to explain to them at Ninewells how I was there covered in blood and feathers.

Anyway, we did manage to get him in reasonably comfortable, as we thought, with the top a wee bit open so he could breathe and I picked him up.

"Are you ok with him like that?"

"No."

"You'll be fine, it's not far."

"I cannot believe I'm doing this."

"You're doing it for me and for him… for us."

"I'm just not sure he'll appreciate it when he wakes up in a strange place."

"You'd better get a move on because you don't want him waking up before you get home. Give him something to eat and I'm sure he'll be fine. Here, take what's left of that fish supper."

"All right, but I'm not putting this down again so just stick it in my jacket pocket and open the door."

"You've got my number, ring me tomorrow and tell me how you both are. And hey… you're a sweetheart."

"I'm an eejit."

So I'm walking down the street praying that the daft bugger doesn't

GUS'N'US

wake up and that nobody sees me. And it was my own fault, I should've known better but the bag was that awkward to carry and I wanted to stay off the main road, so I thought I'd take the short cut down the lane that comes out at the back of my flat. I'd got as far as the middle of the lane, to the bit where it's shadowy and quite narrow between the high walls at the sides.

"Stop right there, pal."

There were two of them stepping out from a gateway in the wall. One was thin and lanky, the other shorter and even in the gloom you could see he had dreadful acne. His plooks were almost fluorescent. Both were wearing the standard neds' uniform of branded trainers and dark hoodies pulled up. It was the lanky one who spoke.

"What you got in the bag?"

"Nothing."

"Let me see in the bag."

"I mean washing."

"Let me see in the bag."

"No."

"Listen, pal, we're going to have your wallet and your phone *and* whatever's in that bag, right?"

"No, no I don't think that would be a very good idea but, tell you what, I'm going to put the bag down right now because it's starting to get heavy."

"Aye, you do that," he said and, turning to his partner in crime, "You look in the bag while I go through his pockets."

Lanky put his hand into my jacket pocket and found the cold remains of a fish supper – "What the fuck?!" – just as Spotty started to bend towards the laundry bag. You'll have heard of 'a bat out of hell', well, 'a seagull out of a laundry bag' is much the same. The big bugger's burst out the bag and headed the boy in the balls, knocked him clean over. And then he's onto him, thrashing him with his wings and pecking at him.

"Get him off me! Get him off me!"

"What the fuck?!"

Lanky's conversation was getting a bit samey. He managed to throw a punch at me and, though I did try to dodge it, he still caught me just under the eye. The other guy was half way to his feet and was trying to scramble away when the big fella gave him a final peck on his retreating arse before turning on Lanky and pulling the same stunt with a perfectly directed head butt in the balls bringing him to his knees before he too managed to scramble his way down the lane, hotly pursued by a whirling dervish of a seagull. I heard a "What the fuck?!" receding into the distance.

And I swear that as that gull walked back up the lane towards me he was smiling. He had a strut to him as well and that's when he became 'Gallus'. He wasn't for getting back in the bag, though I did try the 'Here you are, nice birdie' routine. He just looked at me as if I was nuts. So I just said, "Come on then." And he did, followed me home, nice as you like. He had what was left of the fish supper and a wee bit of toast and settled down in the kitchen for the night. I moved my pots and pans from on top of the kitchen cupboards.

The next day I phoned Margaret and she came straight round when she heard of our wee incident. She made a big fuss about him of course as the hero of the hour but, fortunately, where the boy had hit me I had a nasty blue bruise so I got lots of tea and sympathy too.

It's been a wee while now but she's been round almost every day since and, to be honest, I think she'd be as well just moving in. I'm going to suggest it to her. She's given up being self-employed. And I'm glad – it's different now, now that we're like a couple, almost a family with the big fella. And she's got a job in the chipper. She's gone from being their best customer to being employee of the month. So the big fella gets a fish supper nearly every night which keeps him happy. So does watching the nature programmes on the telly. I bought him the DVD of that *Blue Planet*. He really likes that.

And if anyone ever asks us, "So how did you two get together?" Well, it's quite a story, involving one seagull, two neds, a bottle of cooking oil and a pink laundry bag. You'd never believe it.

Story Wheel Three

TRAPPED

Stuart Wardrop

Cecil stood at the doorway of the restaurant going through the tedious process of bidding farewell to his guests. Some were business colleagues and some were clients. They had all had a fair amount to drink and Cecil marvelled at how easily this turned otherwise intelligent men – and sometimes women – into babbling idiots. Never having been a drinker he couldn't understand their unfocussed silliness, their incoherent ramblings and, worst of all, their occasional fumbled attempts to include him in some sort of bonding ritual that he found quite unnerving.

Suppressing a shudder he turned on his professional smile as he shook hands with the men and air kissed their wives. As clients they were important and had to be networked – and tolerated. He thought for a moment, tasting the word, then nodded to himself. Yes – that was the word – tolerated. He supposed they had some sort of opinion of him. He was well aware of the office gossip – the knowing looks, the sniggers around the photocopier. Fifty something and no wife? This didn't trouble Cecil unduly.

What did trouble him was what he had overheard earlier in the evening. He hadn't meant to eavesdrop. He had stepped outside for a breath of air and from beyond a pair of trees in tubs, borne on a fragrant cloud of tobacco smoke, he'd heard his name. Instinctively he'd stepped back into the foyer and listened. He recognised one of the voices: Frank McCardle's hard-faced wife, Sarah. A policewoman, he'd heard. That would explain much – the bitch. He didn't know the other.

"What d'you reckon to Billy Bunter then?"

"Dunno. Why? Problem?"

"No, just all that smiling and olde worlde charm. A bit creepy don't you think?"

"Mmm. I suppose he is a bit. Funny how we can always tell." A burst of laughter. Cecil stood rooted to the spot. "I suppose that face doesn't help." He felt himself flush. "I'm told he's a wizard with figures though. Saved the company a mint – and that meal was a cracker. No expense spared." There was a shuffling from behind the trees and Cecil had hurried back into the dining-room.

The incident had stayed with him all evening. Was it just his imagination or had some of the wives tensed as he helped them with their coats? As the last couple vanished into a taxi Cecil stood for a time breathing the warm evening air. He turned to allow the gentlest of breezes to cool his face. He tended to sweat a bit, especially in overheated places like this, and it always made his face itch. He was used to alcohol or hypertension getting the blame for his high colour and the blotchy patches, and not the chronic skin disease that had cursed him since childhood.

Scratching at his face Cecil stepped back into the restaurant and examined the bill. Mmm, he thought. I wonder whose tax docket I'll put this one into.

He glanced at his watch. Just after eleven. It was a long time since he'd been in the city centre at this time on a Saturday evening. Looking – but not feeling – a bit out of place in dinner jacket and patent leather shoes he strolled towards South Street.

He wasn't tired, just a bit unsettled. The night was pleasant and he thought he would carry on down to the riverside before collecting his car from the multi-storey.

The street was a kaleidoscope of colour. The warm night sky contributed soft pink, the sodium street lights added their orangey yellow and bright splashes of colour from opening and closing pub doors revealed glimpses of the pulsating activity within. Having been brought up to a wholesome but highly conservative diet Cecil caught his breath at the tang of vinegar and hot fat. His nose wrinkled at other, unidentified smells, and he walked quickly past the darkly exotic aromas hanging heavy outside curry houses.

He felt a sense of detachment, almost as if he was looking through a viewfinder. He was slightly surprised to find that he could cope with the colours – enjoy them even – and if he held his breath for a few paces the smells weren't too bad. It was the noise that got into his head and wouldn't leave. Each pub – and there seemed to be one every few yards – had some sort of raucous music coming from it accompanied by an insistent beat. Sometimes there were voices but Cecil couldn't make out the words and every time a pub door opened a wall of sound reached out and threatened to engulf him.

Crowds of sweaty young men and half-naked – he swallowed hard – young women stood in knots at pub doors smoking and screaming with laughter at the tops of their voices. Cecil had seen the white Transits parked at various junctions and wondered why the police didn't take all these noisy and drunk young people away. Surely there were laws against this sort of behaviour. He felt a vague sense of outrage.

Cecil walked on. As the pubs gradually emptied he watched the goings-on with a growing sense of incredulity. An occupying army of young people surged through the street, constantly changing form and direction like a flock of starlings.

Outside Tesco's he watched fascinated as a group of young women came towards him. Their arms were linked, they were singing and had obviously had a lot to drink. The girls were wearing very little and Cecil felt his face go hot. Sweat prickled his brow and ran down his cheeks. He scratched furiously. Then they were blocking his passage and as he stood there uncertainly they formed a ring with him in the middle. Suddenly a fifty-four-year-old accountant was playing some sort of grotesque Farmer's in his Den with a gang of very drunk teenage girls. As they danced around him squealing with laughter Cecil felt bewildered and quite helpless. He couldn't even find a voice and wished with all his being that he was somewhere else.

The tempo increased and he found himself being spun around by one shrieking girl after the other. He tried again to speak but nothing came and suddenly he felt dizzy. One last spin sent him staggering against one of the girls and the ring broke, pitching him onto the pavement in a whirl of arms and legs. Lying there, dazed, nauseous and terrified, Cecil became aware of faces peering owlishly down at him and fought back the urge to vomit. He lay still, the pavement cool on his cheek and closed his eyes.

"Is he deid?"

"How come he's dressed a' funny? And see his face, Britney. Fuckin hell, it's bealin."

"Is he pished?"

"D'you reckon he's a pervie?"

"Mair like a fuckin penguin – look at that suit."

There was a burst of laughter. The faces loomed large and kept changing shape – like a half remembered hall of mirrors from a childhood amusement park. The faces loomed again.

"Ah'm shair he grabbed ma boob on his way doon."

"Dirty fucker."

"Think he's a poof? Mah ma says the toon centre's fu o them – 'specially Setterdays."

"Mibbe we should introduce him tae Stevie, eh?" More laughter.

"Let's gie him a good kicking – just in case, eh?"

Cecil moaned and instinctively curled into a ball.

"No, girls, let's not, eh?" This was a new voice. Cecil peered up as the shapes dissolved and another face, a larger one, shimmered into view. As the shape bent over him a tiny crucifix on a thin gold chain brushed his cheek.

"Are you OK, my friend?" It was a woman's voice – a humorous voice – a grown-up and reassuring voice. "Are you hurt?"

"No... I... I... I don't think so," Cecil managed to croak. "Are you the police?"

A laugh. "No. My name's Sandie. I'm with the Street Pastors." Sandie paused as if awaiting a response. Cecil looked up at her silently. Sandie went on, "We're volunteers. We come out at weekends just to make sure young people come to no harm." She laughed gently. "I suppose we're quite useful for protecting folk like you as well. You can call the police if you think that's the right thing to do." She looked around, "But it seems to me the kids have gone and as you're all right..."

"All I want to do is to get home. I'm OK now. My car's not far away – in the multi-storey."

"I'll walk with you." Cecil stared at the middle-aged woman. She laughed and the street light glinted off the crucifix. "It's on my way."

Cecil clenched his fists to control his trembling. "No, honestly I'll be alright. Just let me be."

"I insist – just in case you get hijacked again." She smiled and said gently, "It was really only a bit of high spirits, you know – and a bit too much to drink. No harm done."

"No, I suppose not." Cecil was desperate to get away from this place – and this woman.

By concentrating hard he was able to exit the car park and drive home. His earlier feeling of outrage had returned but this time it was accompanied by a growing feeling of humiliation mixed with anger –

and that pastor woman seemed to find it amusing. And what did 'folk like you' mean?

Half an hour later, still shaking, Cecil leaned his forehead on the door as he fumbled with the keypad. Eventually the lock clicked and he stumbled through the hall. He barely made it to the bathroom. The bitter after taste of vomit filled his mouth as he threw himself, trembling, into the sofa's squashy safety.

Eventually Cecil dragged himself off to bed. Nonsense dreams plagued him and several times he awoke bathed in itchy sweat, tangled in damp sheets and with terrifying images banging around in his head. By the time he crawled exhausted from the ruins of the night he knew the script word for word and blow by blow.

No church for him this morning. Cecil simply could not face anything remotely resembling normality. Instead he spent the next hour standing under the shower trying to get his thoughts in order.

It sort of worked. At least he felt clean. Mother would have approved though he flinched at what she would have thought of last night. He wandered the flat restlessly picking things up and putting them down but when mother came into mind she tended to stay and prompt unwelcome thoughts – about himself. Several times Cecil's eyes strayed to where he knew he would find solace, even if he knew it would be temporary. He angrily pushed these thoughts away and tried to focus on safer things. He opened his laptop. Maybe the silvery streams of numbers marching around the screen would work their soothing magic – but not in the same way as... He felt his face heating up and concentrated on the screen.

Cecil tried to focus on the figures but the dark thoughts kept returning. Oh God, he thought. This was what happened before. It was all down to those little bitches last night – and that older one – just like the other times. They had no right. Why didn't I go straight home? Got to concentrate... concentrate. It was hopeless. The secret place in his head – his Pandora's Box – was too strong, and darkly menacing messages flooded his mind. He stared unseeingly at the screen and let his mind freewheel through his past. This was not somewhere he liked to be but anywhere was better than the present.

The tubby, short-sighted little boy with the permanent rash and aversion to sport became a portly, bespectacled adult with the same rash but with an affinity for figures. Sometimes Cecil wasn't sure how he felt about that. He grunted. As if. The solitude he had learned to live with – was comfortable with – but he shuddered to think what would have become of his life without the comfort of numbers. They had taken the place of so much. He had never been comfortable with people, especially women, and relating to men was simply a tedious necessity. He reflected, a little sadly, that his life was built on pretence. The real Cecil had always stayed hidden – except for – sweat prickled his brow. He mustn't think of that. He groaned. It was too late. Last night had released the demons – again – and a price had to be paid.

Cecil closed the laptop and stood, eyes shut and fists tightly clenched. Then he relaxed and walked unsteadily to the spare bedroom. He stood before a steamer trunk that had belonged to his parents – his other Pandora's Box. After staring at it for a long moment Cecil quickly turned the key and flung back the lid.

Closing his eyes tightly he saw himself standing naked beneath an ice-cold waterfall, arms raised, water passing through his head, washing away all thoughts other than what had to be done. After several deep breaths he felt his heart rate slow to a steady thump.

From the trunk he took a small inlaid, wooden box and opened it. He picked out the contents one by one. A velvet hair ribbon from two – no – three years ago. Was it as long ago as that, he thought dreamily? He fingered the soft fabric. Then there was the butterfly with the delicate filigree and coloured stones that felt so smooth, and the tortoiseshell hair thing. A barrette? Was that what it was called? Cecil arranged the articles lovingly on the coffee table and allowed his mind to drift. They would remain there until…

Returning to matters in hand Cecil delved into the trunk and took out a rucksack. He emptied the contents onto the floor. They were every day things, innocuous, almost insignificant – a black cloth bag, a bottle of liquid, a linen pad and a roll of duct tape. The final item though was far from commonplace – a rubber Frankenstein mask.

Waiting for full dark Cecil dressed in his special dark tracksuit, placed the items in a small daysack and left the flat.

Cecil sat at the coffee table as the first sunrays announced the new day. Everything was in its place and he felt calm and in control. He allowed his eyes to caress the ribbon, the butterfly and the barrette. Then he heaved a deep sigh and reverently placed on the table a thin gold chain with a tiny gold crucifix. He stared at them for a moment, then touching them with a fingertip, he placed his head in his hands – and wept.

FAMILY TIES

Fiona Pretswell

The old man shuffled along the muddy track, his plastic-soled slippers soaking up the dampness from the long grass and nettles. The slow gait hid his strong, lithe body, once famed and feared for its fighting skills.

"Och, come on Mary, hurry up. This part's no hard and we're nearly at the steps. I'll gie you a wee kiss at the tap. You always love that."

He trudged on, over the collapsed railings, onto the wood chipped path and up the hill. The wintery sun spilled through the bare trees, casting shadows of giant spiders' webs. Piles of red and golden leaves lay at the side, the top layer rustling and whispering in the wind.

"Will you have a look at that tree, Mary. Storm has blown it right ower. Huge it is. Must be a fair age. How is it you tell the age again? Och yes, that's it. The rings. You count the rings – but it's no cut. The cooncil's nae got roond tae cutting it yet."

The sun was casting a warm ruby glow over the sky as Jack reached the Observatory car park. He stopped to admire the colours, turning eastward to see if, in the increasing shades of twilight, he would catch sight of the first star. The shadows were now long and dark and fine mist had gathered over the Fife hills. Jack shuddered feeling the night chill in the wind.

"Mary, Mary, where are you…? Mary?"

No voice replied. Jack circled around, eyes searching through the dusky light as he felt the dampness ache into his feet. He began to scream Mary's name but only silence answered. The screams subsided to a whimpering. He slumped onto the steps of the Observatory. He didn't know why he was here. Tears fought their way into his eyes and he started to rock himself back and forth.

A young man appeared at the door. His brown hair stood in random spikes and his navy council jumper was all stretched out of shape with bobbles gathering at the elbows. Quickly he hid his cigarette behind his back.

"Ehm... ehm... the Observatory's closed until 4pm today. Ehm, will you no get a bit cold sitting there? Eh'd wait in your car if Eh were you. Oh... you've no car."

Jack turned slowly to stare at the man. His mind was burning. None of his thoughts were connecting to where he was right now. He tried to focus on what he knew.

"My name is Jack. Please phone this number."

He reached into the collar of his jumper and pulled out a heavy silver chain. Dangling on it were two rectangular plates like army dog tags. The young man bent down slowly and reached for the tags. *My Name is Jack Armstrong, please phone my daughter.* And on the reverse side: *Sarah – 0752841165.*

The young man dropped the tags and hurriedly stood up.

"Is this a joke? Is this one o' them council tests like? I ken they do it like. Secret tests of your customer service like. I thought somebody would just ask me about the telescope or the loos or the park. Nae this. Nae offence mate."

Jack just continued to stare out over the car park and rock his body.

"Oh hell, you better just come in and I'll phone the number like."

Sarah sat behind the wheel of her car. The security light from the Observatory barely made a dent in the haar that had descended on Dundee in the past two hours. She didn't want to leave the car, to have to see her father. She looked out and stared as the glow of a cigarette appeared at the door. She waited until the young man had gone back through the door before following him inside.

"Good afternoon. I'm Detective Inspector McCardle."

The young man turned to her. "Er... Eh never called the polis like. He's nae done nothing... and neither have, eh. He's just lost like. Eh think like."

"No, it's..." Sarah looked at his name badge. Always know a name her dad had told her. Always keep it polite. "George... George, I'm sorry. So used to using my formal title. I'm Sarah. You telephoned me. You have my father here."

"Oh, ehm, yeah, like call me Dode. Yeah, he's here."

Dode moved to the side and Sarah saw her dad for the first time

FAMILY TIES

in eighteen months. She felt a pang of guilt. All these years she had tried to get as far away from him as possible, first to Edinburgh and then to the ranks of the police: the antipode of his underworld life. There had been visits until her mum died and then just cards and the occasional phone call. Having a 'collector' as a father wouldn't have gone down well. Luckily for her he'd never been caught; never left a black stain on her prospects. She watched him as he sat there, his shoulder wrapped in a council fleece, the hems of his trousers caked in dried mud.

Jack straightened himself up and looked at her. "Hello Sarah. I got a bit confused for a while. Dode here helped me."

Sarah turned away. "Excuse me, Dode, but where are his coat and shoes?"

"Wasn't wearing anything else like. Found him like that."

"How long was he sitting there?"

"Don't know. Went out for a smoke... I mean to check the car park before opening and there he was. He was shouting something about Mary."

"Mary?"

"Yep."

Sarah moved over and sat down beside Jack, her leather-gloved hand gently taking his. "Dad, why were you here? Mum's dead. You do know that."

"Eugh... creepy like... looking for a dead person. Did he think this was the cemetery path like?"

"No. He has Alzheimer's. He forgets things. I'll take him home now."

Jack had been lucid in the car on the way home. He asked Sarah about her job, her husband Frank and Edinburgh. He'd even remembered the name of the wee Jack Russell that she'd bought two years ago. But Sarah knew that these times would not last as she opened the door and saw the state of the house. Newspapers and egg boxes were piled up on the kitchen cabinets, the small bin was reeking and greasy pools smudged the surfaces. Jack followed her in, pulled off his wet slippers and slouched down onto the couch.

"Make us a cuppy please, Mary love. That was a long day at work. I'm fair puffed. A wee bit of shortie would go down a treat too."

Sarah just nodded, rolled up her sleeves and put the kettle on.

Fiona Pretswell

Later when Sarah could hear her dad humming away to himself as he had his bath, she finished drying up the tea dishes and let herself sink down into her favourite armchair. It was red velvet, now worn through, embroidered with flowers in green and pink, the high back topped by a fluted design. When Sarah had been a child she had always imagined that it was a throne, a magical place to sit. Occasionally, when her dad was out she would sneak in and sit on it. The rest of the time it remained empty. Only her father's special visitors were allowed to use it. The visitors she always wanted to meet but each time she was shooed upstairs.

Sarah would sit on the landing and listen to the voices. She would hear her father's west coast tones occasionally but mainly he seemed to listen. The voice she loved the best was that of the dark-haired man. She caught a glimpse of him only once. Tanned with black hair swept back off his face, he wasn't tall but he commanded the room. He had smiled at Sarah as her mother had ushered him out of the room. It was years later that she learnt his name.

Sarah fidgeted on the chair. There was something hard under the cushion. She moved and lifted it but there was nothing visible. As she went to plump it up, hoping that would remove whatever was wrong, she realised that the lump was inside the cushion itself. She pulled at the zip. Its teeth were stiff and the zip snagged a few times but eventually it opened. She rummaged around inside and hauled out a small black book. Flicking through it she saw lists of dates, names and amounts of money. Just then her dad started down the stairs. Quickly she replaced the cushion and settled herself on the couch, flicking the TV on as she did so. She placed the book on the coffee table, half hidden under a newspaper.

The evening settled into a quiet silence broken only by the voices from the various programmes her dad was watching. Distracted by the adverts he would flick over and continue to watch a different channel until the next ad break. Sarah didn't care. Her mind was too busy wondering about the book and its contents. She wanted to look at it, study it, hoping it was what she wanted – a list of all her Dad's connections and contacts. If it was that, then it could be the catalyst she needed to change her life.

"Would you like a cup of something, dad?"

"No thanks, Mary, but if you're up I'll hae a wee dram."

She picked up her mug from earlier and went into the kitchen.

FAMILY TIES

Once the kettle was on she started to hunt for the whisky.

"Where's your bottle Dad? I can't see it."

"It's through here where I always keep it. Just bring a glass and the water jug, love."

Sarah heard the couch creak as her dad stood up and moved to get the whisky and then the noise of things being tidied up. She continued to make her tea and prepare the rest of the things on the wicker and glass tray. She returned to find her dad sitting on the chair, bottle on the cleared table and hands clutching onto the black book. She stiffened and forced a smile, walking to the table where she carefully placed the tray before turning to look at her father.

"Mary, Mary you've found it. Why didn't you tell me?"

"Found what, Jack?" Sarah was trembling. She wanted to rush over and grab the book from his hands but didn't dare. She needed to hear what her dad would say.

"My book, Mary, my book. You always knew what I needed, didn't you?"

Sarah watched her dad. His eyes were focused on a distant point in time as his lips curled into a gentle smile. Sarah reached for the remote and muted the television. The silence in the room was broken only by the ticking of the old mahogany mantle clock. She held her breath, anticipation burning in her lungs. Her father flicked through the pages, shaking and nodding his head as he remembered his old life.

"What exactly did you keep in your book? Maps of where all the bodies were buried?" Sarah forced herself to laugh lightly as she spoke, hoping that she hadn't pushed her father too far.

"Och, Mary, I thought you never wanted to know as long as the bills were paid on time and the polis never turned up at the door. Not exactly maps, love, more dates and names and transactions. But you're right about the bodies. None my doing though. I never went that far. I just helped in the clean up and was paid wisely for it."

Sarah exhaled. A cold sweat was enveloping her neck and shoulders.

"May I?"

Her father handed over the book.

"What was the name of that nice young Italian man who used to come around? It was something like Lucca. I wonder what happened to him."

Fiona Pretswell

"Luccini. His name was Luccini. He knew how to work in this business. He got too big to need me around."

Sarah studied the small leather-bound book. The pages were well thumbed and the ink smudged in places. A strip of sellotape had turned yellowy brown as it had dried out; the item it had once been used to keep in place was long gone. Most of the pages were filled. Sarah recognised her father's small precise handwriting. Folded and tucked into the back was a clipping from the *Tully*. It was a photograph taken inside a club – one of the 'girls' nite out' pictures. Sarah didn't recognise any of the women but she did know who the man behind the bar was – Luccini. Her father started to snore gently. Sarah stood. Taking the blanket from the back of the couch she carefully covered her dad before turning off the TV.

It was chilly outside. The haar from earlier still hung in the air, blanking out the stars. Sarah took out her phone and sent a couple of text messages. While waiting for the replies she sat on the wooden bench and supped the coffee she'd made, thinking about what her next move should be… could be. Her phone vibrated and she read her replies An excited shiver ran through her body. Finally she could be who she always wanted to be. This would be the first move to her new life. All it would take would be one call and a lot of luck. She hoped her father would be proud. She dialled the number. The phone seemed to ring for an eternity.

"Prime. How can I help you?"

"Luccini please."

"Who wants him?"

"Tell him it's an old friend."

Bland pop music could be heard as Sarah was put on hold. She was grateful that the person hadn't just hung up on her. After JLS had wooed her with a song a smooth voice replaced the music.

"So 'old friend', what can I do for you?"

Sarah took a deep breath. This was it. No turning back now.

"Good evening, Señor Luccini. My name is Sarah, Jack Armstrong's daughter. I don't know if you'll remember me."

Sarah could hear Luccini breathing before he answered her.

"Miss Armstrong. What a pleasure to hear from you. What can I do for you? You must be all grown up now. If I remember correctly you were slightly older then my eldest."

FAMILY TIES

"I'm honoured that you remember me. I have a proposition for you. I'm hoping to, how shall I say it, take over the family business and I wanted to know if we could work together."

CROSS

Fiona Duncan

A quiet room in an unnamed building. Shutters block out a wintry, watery sun. The walls and ceiling are painted black. So is the woodwork. And the floor. Recessed lights converge on a figure. He is fixed to a cross mounted on one wall, his arms and legs held apart, tightly bound by leather cords. His head slumps on his chest so that only the top is visible. Black hair, dripping down and down, the ends straggling slow, bloody drops onto the floor beneath him. He breathes. Shallow gasps with enough time between for a spectator to wonder if. To wonder. His chest deflates, is still, but then, another defiant whisp of breath. Every rib shows beneath skin the colour of wax candles.

Opposite, under a wall-mounted digital clock which blinks green as each minute ticks away, a man sits on an immaculate grey sofa. His body is upright, his back straight. His black suit is sharp edges, his shirt a brilliant white. His eyes open, blink. He is considering, weighing up this and that. Deciding. The ringing of a bell breaks his concentration, an intrusion from... elsewhere. He frowns, then, standing up, pulls his cuffs straight and adjusts his tie. The door smoothly closes and locks behind him as he leaves, moving towards his other world.

In the dark room, the clock clicks down, while bright beads of blood drip monotonously onto black boards.

Inside his head is white and haze. And a red dullness, a perfect point which is pain. His arms and shoulders bear his entire body weight. Cruel thorns pierce the skin of his brow, and he knows who has done this, who has placed him here in this room, on this cross. His head throbs. His eyes remain closed, the lids leaded. To lift these seems impossible. And what would be the point? He knows this room. Black. Shutters. Clock. Grey sofa. Lights. Door. He knows the room. He's been here before. Many times. He breathes, shallow sips of stagnant air, feeling the constriction, the disastrous crush of his chest. Breathe. Concentrate. Focus. Breathe. He moves his feet slightly, holding his arms and shoulders stiffly, every movement a burning flare of agony. Focus. Breathe. Weary beyond speech, he lifts his head slowly, so slowly. The clock ticks down its relentless minutes. An age passes. He opens one eye, a brief flash of blue, then gone. Again. Both eyes. His skin is torn by the crown's jagged spikes. These wounds ache still, but the pain now feels far away. The fog in his head is lifting, clearing, and intently he stares at the door with mingled hope and fear. Luccini will be back. To talk. To question.

He's ready now. Ready to tell him the truth.
The harsh pulse of laboured breathing.
The clock.
These are the only sounds.
For now.

"I don't like what you're doing."
Two men talking, one leaning against a gleaming, mahogany bar, playing idly with a twist of sugar, the other behind the bar, polishing a glass. Italian, shot through with streaks of gold. Before replying, he places it delicately on a shelf, admiring the perfect symmetry he has created. The men are alone at the bar in Prime. The club is empty apart from two girls whispering in the deep leather seats before the fire and a solitary man intent on his laptop screen. No one can hear the men as they talk, but still, it is a cryptic reply.

"No. It is quite... unpleasant, Mr Wiseman. But you want information. You ask me to... extract it. You have changed your mind, perhaps? You wish me to release him?"

Joe Wiseman doesn't answer. He doesn't look at his bar manager, Thomas Luccini. Instead, he surveys the club, quiet at this time of day, a fading afternoon in November. Outside, the streets of Dundee will be slick and grey with rain, the sky lowering, darkness hovering, rolling in gradually across the river. He turns to Luccini who waits in perfect silence.

"I want to know why he stole from me. I want to know who else was involved. I want to know how far it's gone. I want..."

He stops, hesitating, vaguely troubled by what he is about to say.

"And you want... revenge. To punish those responsible."
Luccini leans forward to stare directly into the uneasy eyes of his boss.

"Quite right, Mr Wiseman. An eye for an eye… Leave it to me. I will get you results."

Wiseman nods slowly, but his teeth are clenched and his hands grip the edges of the bar, tightly.

"Fine. But not like last time with your fucking Edgar Allan Poe antics. The guy insulted you, Thomas. Big fucking deal. Words, Thomas, words. You should have ignored him. That's part of your job. Instead we had the police crawling all over the club and the gym. We were closed for two days, for fuck's sake! Just lucky for you they didn't find anything."

Luccini allowed himself a small smile of satisfaction at the memory of his revenge. Almost a year ago and still nobody knew what had happened to that Lochee scum and his tart of a girlfriend. No one except Luccini and his sons and daughter. And, of course, Mr Wiseman. The bones had been long ago disposed of, ground down and added to the cement in one of Mr Wiseman's Waterfront Projects, the new forensic building opposite the Apex Hotel. His son, Alessandro, had quite a sense of humour.

"It was not luck, Mr Wiseman, with respect. It was expert planning. It was teamwork. It was the perfect…"

His voice faded, leaving Wiseman to fill in that last word. Murder. Luccini knew what his boss wanted from the man in the room above. Information. Answers. The truth. And Luccini would provide these. In his own way. In his own time. And Wiseman knew that.

"Change the subject. How long before you have answers? I can't trust anyone, the situation just now. Business is suffering. And he'll be missed. You don't have much longer. The last thing we want is his nosy friends coming here. Or any polis pricks from Bell Street."

Wiseman lowered his voice as a customer approached the bar. Luccini poured a perfect Peroni, inclining his head slightly as he handed over the beer. He waited until the man was out of earshot before replying smoothly.

"Leave it to me. He is ready to talk. I can tell. I will return to the room above at two when the bar closes. Then he will tell me everything. And I will tell you. Or you can watch the whole thing yourself from your office. James and Alessandro have set up cameras in the room, linked to the security system. Nothing could be easier to arrange."

Wiseman shuddered. He swallowed his whisky, wiped his

mouth and stood up.

"And after?" he asked.

"You must decide, Mr Wiseman. Perhaps after hearing what he has to say?"

Joe Wiseman made no reply. Luccini helped him on with his Vicuna overcoat, observed gravely as he fussed with his black cashmere scarf and pulled on his gloves.

"Arrivederci, Mr Wiseman. Till later, then."

Luccini watched until Wiseman had left the club, then made himself a macchiato. A break. Then to work. It would be a long night. But rewarding. Yes, that was the word. Rewarding.

"Take him down, James."

Luccini sat on the grey sofa, perfectly centred, his legs together, feet precisely placed. Across from him, a chair straight-backed, oak. He waited while, in silence, his son lowered the cross, loosened the wrist straps and helped the man to stand.. A groan. Circulation returned to cramped muscles. The clock ticked on while two men stared silently at a third.

"On the chair, James."

Luccini watched as his son, almost tenderly, helped the man to sit down. "Give him water."

James held a bottle to the man's lips. Trembling, he drank, drops like crystal tears glittering as they dripped down his chin, his chest.

"Well, well, Father. It is most regrettable that we find ourselves in this situation, is it not? You know, of course, why you're here?"

There is no answer. The clock moves round. Then, a voice, tired, cracked round the edges by pain.

"I know, Luccini. I know."

"The crown, Father. Mr Wiseman sent you on a mission of trust. To attain this object. And you succeeded. You brought it back to us. The plan perfectly executed, the plan we pored over in this very room, making sure that it was perfect… you did it, Father. You remember that night? The same night that poor little child was found on Balgay Hill. Dead. Murdered. But we didn't know that then. We only knew we had the crown. Mr Wiseman was a happy man. He rewarded you well. And Saint Aloysius too, if I remember rightly. And now… well, you can imagine his disappointment…"

Luccini's voice trailed off, his eyes closing for a few seconds, like a man in prayer, then suddenly snapping them open, he clicked his fingers and pointed at Father John's head, at the crown.

"Remove it. Wear gloves. Place it on the plinth here, James. Yes. Beside the other."

Two crowns of thorns, old wood, scarred and battered, the thorns sharp still. Identical apart from the fresh stains of blood blotched on the one which had been removed from the priest's head.

"Now, Father John – which is the true crown of Christ? The crown Mr Wiseman desired above everything? The one reputed to contain thorns from the original worn by Our Lord? One you gave us which we took in good faith, believing you, taking your word, trusting you. The other was found in your study, Father. By your cleaner, Agnes, who, as you know, also works in Prime. Intrigued, she raised the subject with me. Two crowns? One on show in Prime, alongside our other… rare artefacts. One in a priest's study? You can see our problem, Father. You understand why we have… questions?"

The priest raised his head. Dried scabs of blood cracked as he spoke, slowly, out of a blank haze. His body felt… other… distant. As if it didn't belong to him. He spoke into a grey mist, Luccini hovering like a dark angel, listening intently, his head inclined.

"Try it on. Put it on. The one you found. But don't blame me. I wanted to protect…"

His voice failed. His head slumped. Exhausted, beyond speech, he sat, defeated.

Luccini narrowed his eyes. He assessed the situation. Further persuasion would achieve nothing. The man was done for now, a pitiful, broken thing. He might recover. He might not. It meant nothing to Luccini. Betrayal should be punished. Harshly.

"You going to try it , Dad?"

James looked expectant and intrigued.

"Why not?" replied Luccini.

James lifted the crown of thorns, placed it on his father's head and waited.

A cell. Night time. A warm wind smelling of sand and spices, and the sound of women wailing. A man: long, matted hair; thin, ascetic face. He is crying. Someone has forsaken him. Sacrificed his life. He doesn't want to die. Not here.

CROSS

Not now. Even if it is for the Greater Good. His father is wrong. He is begging his father to save him, not to let him be crucified. Crucify the thief, he is saying, anyone, just spare his life. For how could it work? One man. To save the sins of all people, through all time? It would never work. His father was deluded. Mad. Crazed with power. No! He didn't want to die alone on a cross derided, taunted by ignorant soldiers, gaming for his cloak, waiting for him to take a last shuddering, agonised breath. Mankind could save itself. He wanted to live...

Luccini ripped the crown from his head and spun it from him. He stood sweating and trembling in the black room, staring at the priest with horrified eyes.

THE CLEANER AND THE CAT

Ann-Marie Aslen

Aggie paused a moment to catch her breath. She'd fallen asleep on the bus and missed her stop. Now she had to hurry back down the street so she wouldn't be late for work. The early mornings were a killer that's for sure. Get up at five, leave George his breakfast in the kitchen, lay his pills out so he'd know which ones to take, and put his glasses on top of the paper. Then get dressed and catch the 6.30 bus to work. Clean the pubs in the Students' Union then hurry on over to her afternoon cleaning job. The old priest she cleaned for was a nice enough chap but he did have a lot of fragile looking stuff. Aggie was always terrified she'd wind up breaking some of it: her arthritis meant her hands weren't as steady as they used to be. She'd never be able to pay for it; her cleaning jobs and meagre pension were all they had to live on.

If only George hadn't claimed those Pension credits. The DSS had overpaid them and seized George's pension to pay them back. She'd said at the time it seemed like a lot of money to be getting but George had told her not to worry. So she hadn't. Right up until she'd gone to the post office to withdraw their money to pay a bill and found the account almost empty. She'd been lucky to get these part- time jobs, and she was grateful, but at the same time resentful that a 78-year-old woman couldn't stop working for fear they'd starve. George, bless him, at 87 simply couldn't work. His leg had never been right after the war and crippling arthritis had set in twenty-odd years ago. Aggie paused again at the glass-fronted entrance to the Students' Union and caught her breath. Pasting a smile on her face, she entered.

The other cleaners were already getting their cleaning supplies out of the cupboard when Aggie arrived downstairs and hung her coat and bag in the cleaners' cloakroom.

"You're late this morning," Ruth called cheerfully. "Something happen?" Aggie shook her head and her smile became genuine. She liked Ruth. The big chubby woman was their gaffer and always had a joke and a smile for everyone. She also handed out overtime like confetti whenever the students had a big bash on, like Halloween or the Christmas parties.

"Ruth, is there any chance of any overtime this weekend? I mean Halloween seems to go on all weekend, lots of partying so…"

"There should be but some of the others have asked as well. I might not have much for you. Why? What's wrong, Aggie?"

"Well, it's just that George had a bad spell with his angina so I had to put the heating on for a bit and, well, the bill came… Just a bit of overtime, that's all I need."

"Of course, I'll make sure you get an extra shift, Aggie. What about Michael or Janet? Can't they help out their dad a bit?"

Aggie kept her eyes resolutely fixed to the floor so she couldn't see the sympathy in the other woman's. "They've got their own families to be thinking of. Janet's just got her third grandchild and Michael's youngest has lost his job again and had to move back home. They don't have anything to spare and we wouldn't ask. It's not right, asking your own kids for money. They need it more than we do."

"Of course they do. Bad news about Michael's youngest. Here's hoping he gets another job soon," soothed Ruth. "Anyway, grab your bucket. We're all cleaning the big one today. The students had a pre-Halloween bash last night and it's pretty bad. All hands on deck!"

Aggie grabbed her wheeled bucket, mop and floor cleaner and turned to follow Ruth and the other cleaners. Her heart gave a little lurch as she saw Alice watching her, a secretive smile on the other woman's face. Aggie forced a smile as she passed, Alice falling into step behind her. Ever since last Thursday Aggie had been on tenterhooks. She'd had to go back to the cloakroom for some asprin and she'd seen Alice go through Keira's bag. Aggie had thought nothing of it until later when Keira had announced that she'd lost a twenty pound note from her handbag. Aggie had immediately glanced across at Alice to see the middle-aged woman staring coldly straight back at her. She had wanted to tell Ruth what she'd seen but Alice always could out-argue anyone, twisting things to suit herself. Aggie had never been very confrontational and, terrified she would lose her life-line job, had said nothing. All week Alice had been making remarks about how hard up Aggie was and how hard it must be for her to make ends meet. Now, after that disquieting smile from Alice, she was wondering if she'd done the right thing.

Ann-Marie Aslen

Aggie wrestled her bucket upstairs to the huge dance floor. Caked-in spilled drinks, vomit and sticky shoe-prints were everywhere. She could see why Ruth had wanted everyone upstairs. It was going to take a *lot* of cleaning. Just then she noticed the long halloween curtains billowing in one corner.

"Oh great, someone's left a window open and the floor will be *concrete* after all the rain yesterday," complained Samantha. The young mum strode forward and swept the curtain aside. Behind it, a very drunk couple were frenetically having sex. The cleaners gaped as the young man said, "Excuse me! We're not done yet!" before dragging the curtain back into place.

Ruth looked at her watch. "He gets two minutes."

Samantha started to snigger as Alice instantly started having the vapours. "Well, I never! I can't believe that... Ooohhh!"

Ruth leapt to catch Alice before her skinny legs gave out. "Maybe you'd better go back downstairs and start cleaning the toilets," she said dryly.

Aggie watched her go with misgivings. Suddenly the drape whisked open and the barely clad teenagers staggered out. "All done," slurred the boy. "Cheers!" Leading the semi-conscious girl by the hand he lurched for the stairs. Ruth beckoned Samantha forward. "See they get out without breaking any legs, okay? Then head back here." The blonde nodded and hurried out. "Okay, ladies, you know what to do!" called Ruth. Aggie filled her bucket with soapy water and grimly attacked the mess.

"Finished already? I wish I had more like you," Ruth said, smiling at Aggie. "Can you do me a favour? Go check on Alice. She should have finished those toilets ages ago. Thanks, you're a love."

Aggie smiled tiredly and hefted her bucket and mop back downstairs to the cleaning cupboard. Puting them inside she jumped as something caressed her ankles with a soft mew.

"Oh! Isis! You didn't half make me jump, kitty. How did you get in here? You know you're not allowed." Bright green eyes stared back at Aggie as she made a clumsy grab for the white cat. Isis instantly darted to her left and into the cleaner's cloakroom.

Aggie followed as fast as her knees would let her. "I don't have any cheese sandwiches to share with you today, puss. You know Ruth

THE CLEANER AND THE CAT

will be mad if she sees you. Let me put you outside."

Isis stared back at her from her perch on the bench next to Aggie's handbag. Putting out a creamy paw, she delicately toppled the bag onto the floor. Tissues, keys and a myriad of empty purses spilled from it. Aggie put disbelieving hands to her mouth. The little cat jumped down and sniffed at one of the purses, letting out a cat sneeze of disgust. Pattering over to one of half a dozen plastic buckets she sniffed and sneezed again. Glancing at the old woman Isis let out a plaintive meow and began pawing at the bucket.

Aggie picked up the offending purse in a daze and gingerly sniffed at it. It did have a familiar scent, one not normally associated with faux leather. Gingerly kneeling beside the cat she pulled the bin bags from the bucket, picked up a familiar can of air freshener and sniffed again. The smells were the same. A half-hidden Gucci purse in the bottom confirmed whose bucket this was. Not daring to think about what she was doing, Aggie opened it and stared at all the stolen tens and twenties stuffed inside..

"Oh, she set me up. What am I going to do?" wailed Aggie as she met the cat's gaze. Isis's eyes seemed to grow larger before the cat broke the spell and ran to the purses. Batting with her paws she quickly flicked one over to the bucket and softly mewed again. Aggie's face slowly wrinkled in a smile. "Good thinking puss. But let's hurry," she added as the sound of voices began to echo down the corridor.

Aggie was putting on her coat when the other cleaners walked in, Alice among them. Rita instantly noticed Isis lurking under the bench. "What's that bloody animal doing in here again?"

Aggie feined innocence as she glanced under the bench. "I don't know Ruth. I'll take it outside with me though."

A sudden wail of "Nooooo! Where is it?!" echoed in the small room. Everyone turned to see Samantha turn her handbag upside down and shake the contents onto the bench. "My purse!" she gasped, "it's gone! It had my shopping money for the week in it! That was all the money I had. What am I going to do?"

"Not to worry, Sammy, I can lend you twenty quid," replied Heather, her ham-like hands rummaging through the depths of her bag. "Hang on a sec, can't seem to find mine either."

The other cleaners all ripped open their bags to find their

purses missing, Alice acting her part with aplomb.

"Maybe it's Aggie," Alice suggested with a shrewish glint to her eye. "After all, she hasn't said if her purse is missing. And we all know she needs the cash. Why don't you show us your bag?"

Ruth gave Alice a nasty look. "Aggie, love, I don't believe her but if you'd just show us your bag we can get on with finding the real thief."

Aggie sighed in mock resignation before emptying her bag onto the bench. Alice's look of triumph quickly faded into panic as only Aggie's purse was revealed. Snatching it up she opened it to reveal the grand total of eight pounds seven pence. "I... I don't understand," she muttered, tossing the battered purse back onto the bench.

Ruth glared daggers at Alice. "I'm so sorry, Aggie. Aren't you sorry, Alice? What's that bloody animal doing now?"

Everyone turned to see the white cat paw at a bucket before meowing insolently at them. Ruth stamped over to shoo it away and stopped as she noticed a purse peeking out from under some bin bags. Cautiously she tipped the bucket over with her foot. A cascade of bin bags and stolen purses flooded the floor, a tin of air freshener rolling amongst them. Ruth turned to look at Alice, her eyes narrowing dangerously. "Care to explain, love?"

"That's not mine!" spluttered Alice indignantly, eyes darting around the room like scared mice.

"Oh yeah?" challenged Heather, her enormous bosom heaving with rage. "I remember the bloody fuss you made when I used the last of the air freshener and your toilets had to stink for the week. You always brought your own in after that. Some minging thing that smelt like a bear shat in some lavender." Her yellow croc nudged the offending can. "That's the one. You never let anybody use it. And that knockoff Gucci purse is yours. I remember you bragging about it."

Samantha reached down and picked up the purse as Alice lunged for it. Opening it up to reveal the wad of money crushed inside she glared at Alice.

Heather's meaty hand clamped down on Alice's shoulder as Ruth flipped open a mobile phone. "Time for the polis I think. You'd better go, love. No sense you getting caught up in this hoo-haa. And take the cat with you."

Aggie nodded her thanks, shot a meaningful smile at Alice whose eyes widened in dismay and shuffled towards the exit. Isis

THE CLEANER AND THE CAT

danced in front of her, tail held high in a victory salute.

"You certainly saved my bacon, little puss. Thank you," Aggie said once they were safely outside.

Isis mewed softly again then shot off across the street in blur of white. Aggie put her cold hands into her coat pocket. Feeling the twenty quid she'd taken from Alice's coat she had a momentary pang of guilt. "What's sauce for the goose," she muttered as she made her way to the bus stop.

Story Wheel Four

NO HIDING PLACE

Catherine Maidment

Everyone it seemed had loved Tom, Diane's husband. At his funeral, Dundee Crematorium was packed, with standing room only at the back – almost as many as there had been in Perth when Tom's cousins died, leaving behind poor little Caro. Susan, Diane's sister, had been upset then too, of course, but on this occasion she sobbed right through the service. When Diane remarked about it afterwards she was horrified in case her sister should suspect anything wrong and since then she'd been jumpy whenever the phone rang. She felt she was the only one who knew what Tom was really like. And she suspected that fatal car crash was no accident.

Even Brian, her husband, had noticed something was amiss.

"Just 'cos you did that bereavement counselling course doesn't mean you have to treat Diane with kid gloves," he chided her. "Believe me, she's OK. She went to the works' party last month and was up dancing most of the time."

"I know," replied Susan. "She's really amazing. But I can't help feeling it hasn't hit her yet."

"If you say so," Brian said, picking up his paper again.

Susan was vexed with herself for feeling guilty. She remembered when Tom first started to pay her attention. He'd begun by waiting outside her office to give her a lift home when she was tired. He was so considerate she'd felt quite envious of Diane. He'd open the car door for her and put her bag in the boot, always behaving like the perfect gentleman. If she was honest with herself she did find him rather attractive. She felt she ought to have known better. No man goes out of his way to give you lifts nearly every night without expecting something back.

Then one night he'd stopped the car in a quiet street and covered his face with his hands.

"I'm worried about Diane," he confided. "She's going through at least a couple of bottles of gin a week."

"What?" asked Susan. "She used to hardly touch the stuff. What's wrong with her?"

"Wish I knew," he replied. "Most nights she falls asleep in front of the tele with her mouth open. I have to help her to bed."

Susan had been really worried and tried phoning her sister of an evening to ascertain if her speech was slurred. Usually Tom answered and he'd say, "She's too far gone to come to the phone. You're better to phone in the morning but don't let on I told you."

Susan never did find Diane the worse for drink but she had no reason to disbelieve Tom. She'd told Brian about it but predictably he'd just advised her to leave her sister alone, before getting back to the mid-week match on the TV. Susan watched him slump on the sofa and sighed.

After the funeral Susan spent more and more time over at Diane's, anxiously watching everything she did.

"Oh God," she thought, "if she knew what Tom was really like she'd definitely have an excuse to drink."

But apart from a half empty bottle of Famous Grouse that remained untouched in the kitchen cupboard, there was never any sign of drink in the house. Diane looked as she always had, hair tinted and regularly blow-dried, dressed neatly, even if the style was a little old-fashioned. Had Tom lied about it?

Susan had felt sorry for Tom about Diane's drinking. It couldn't be fun living with someone who got drunk every night. Tom deserved better. She had hoped it helped him to have someone to confide in. She still didn't think too much about the attention he was paying her even when the presents started. He was subtle at first, a small box of sweets to thank her for listening, a bunch of carnations. Why had she not seen what was happening and ended the whole thing then? She supposed she had been flattered. After all, when had Brian ever given her flowers? Then Tom had kissed her and confessed he was in love with her. Claimed he loved both sisters equally. How could he? But he was pretty convincing.

She'd tried to resist but Tom was very persistent. She'd had to be very firm to stop him phoning her at work. Colleagues might get suspicious. They were very discreet; either meeting out of town or at his house only when he was sure Diane was definitely not going to return for hours. Surely neither Brian nor Diane need ever know. That way, no one would get hurt. She could not help feeling guilty though, especially when they used Tom and Diane's bedroom. Diane had been so good to her ever since their mother had died three years ago. She'd no other close family and could not bear the thought of falling out with her only sister. And if Diane had a drink problem, something must be upsetting her.

Susan endured several weeks of disturbed sleep, racked by guilt about what was happening and terrified of being found out. Meanwhile, Tom kept giving her presents, including a sapphire ring, perfume and a beautiful silver brooch, all of which had to be hidden from Brian. The brooch was the final straw. It was an abstract design, but if you looked closely, it was made of the numerals 1, 2 and 3. Tom said it meant 'I love you' and that he had designed it and had it made especially for her. She knew then that things had gone too far and she made up her mind to call a halt.

At that stage, Tom tried what she could only think of as emotional blackmail. Said he would die without her. Said she was the only person who kept him going. Somehow she found the strength to tell him she would not see him alone again. He said it would kill him, but she didn't believe him. At least, not until that horrendous crash on the A9.

She'd never know what truly happened that night. It was a dark, wet night but no cause could be found for the single car crash and it was recorded as accidental. Susan desperately wanted to believe it was. Diane seemed concerned that Tom's mobile phone was never found in the car. She had discussed with Susan the possibility of him being sent out on a special delivery for his work.

"He might have been trying to text me when it happened," she said. "He always let me know if he was going to be late."

"Yes, he was always thoughtful," replied Susan, "but Tom surely wouldn't be texting while he was driving." Privately, she thought the loss of the mobile and its memory might be a blessing. All she could do was pray that Diane never found out the truth. And hope that Tom had not left anything at all in the way of evidence.

A few months passed and it seemed she had got away with it. Then Diane announced she had decided to sell her house. Even though a four bedroom house was excessively spacious for one person, since her daughters were both long married, she'd expected Diane to take more time to think about it. And surprisingly, considering the current state of the housing market, the sale was finalised in less than three

NO HIDING PLACE

weeks. A grinning Diane told Susan she'd managed to reserve the last of the new luxury flats in Ballinard Road.

"What will you do with all that stuff?" Susan asked. The house was originally Tom's parents' home and they had been great collectors, so there were huge pieces of furniture in every room. Great mahogany dressers were laden with antiques, with valuable old dolls and porcelain figures on all the high surfaces. The lower cupboards were packed with crystal glasses and china dinner services. It was certainly a house full of potential hiding places. If there was anything Tom had secreted away, now was the time it would be discovered.

As the elder sister, Diane had always been confident and capable. She was no different now. She energetically set to clearing and 'downsizing'. Every time Susan visited, there were several boxes of items for her to take to Oxfam. Although Tom's accident had been sudden, Diane said she had discussed matters with him years ago. A valuator from an auction house in Perth visited and catalogued all the valuables. The firm sent men to pack up the items, including the heavy furniture, ready for the saleroom. To Susan's amazement, most of the big pieces could be taken apart into smaller units. She had wondered how they could be managed through the narrow doorways and down the stairs.

Tom's bureau was a lovely item, with the oak in wonderful swirly patterns on the outside of the fold-down writing part and the inside all fitted into little cubby holes. There were three drawers under the desk part and a glass-fronted bookcase on top.

"Are you sending Tom's bureau to the saleroom?" asked Susan.

"Well, yes," replied Diane. "Unless of course you want it?"

"I'd love it!" Susan exclaimed. "But isn't it worth a lot of money?"

Diane explained that only fifteen years ago, it might have sold for a couple of hundred pounds but now people wanted desks suitable for their computers.

"Right enough," said Susan. "I don't really have room for it in my house either, but I'll help you empty it out."

However, Diane had already done that. When Diane went to put the kettle on, Susan quickly searched for hidden compartments, starting guiltily when Diane popped her head back to ask what she wanted to drink.

Over their coffee, Diane told Susan about some receipts she'd found in the bureau. Susan's mouth went completely dry and she felt herself stiffen as she waited for Diane to go on.

"Yes. You know how he always bought me jewellery for my birthdays and Christmas? He kept all the receipts. I'd no idea he'd spent so much on me over the years."

"You're very lucky," said Susan, inwardly hoping it was only receipts for Diane's presents that had been saved. Surely Tom had destroyed the others. "Did I ever show you this special brooch Tom designed himself?" asked Diane, producing a small gold brooch with an abstract design. "If you look closely, it's made up of the numbers 1, 2 and 3. It means 'I love you'."

"What a treasure!" exclaimed Susan. 'What a creep!' she thought. 'Same as mine but in gold.' Thankfully, she'd never worn her silver one and would now have to get rid of it. She wondered briefly what the goldsmith had thought about Tom's order. Perhaps it was usual to buy gold for the wife and silver for the mistress? She thought she'd read that somewhere.

Susan came round very early on the moving day and kept looking round checking everything. Diane seemed in quite a happy mood, joking and laughing. She'd obviously been busy for the last couple of days as she was so organised. Everything was sorted into labelled boxes, the cat was boarded at her daughter's, the freezer and all the cupboards emptied. When the men arrived, Diane calmly gave them directions and offered cans of coke and biscuits when they looked hot and thirsty after moving most of the heavier items.

Once they had loaded the van Susan and Diane walked around, their footsteps echoing as they checked the empty rooms. Susan felt melancholy and expected her sister to be tearful. Surely there must be so many memories in the family home she'd shared with Tom for almost thirty years and where she'd raised her two daughters. But Diane was made of sterner stuff than she had thought. She seemed quite calm and actually smiled as she locked the door for the last time.

At the new flat, the sisters shared the sandwiches and coffee Susan had brought and then, right on cue, the removal men arrived. By the time they left Susan felt exhausted, physically and emotionally, but of course she stayed to help Diane make up her bed and unpack at least some of the kitchen essentials.

Although Susan knew that Tom and Diane's house had been completely emptied and that Diane had been through everything before the move she took some weeks to relax and recover from the emotional strain she had been suffering.

Then one Saturday morning she got a phone call from a tearful-sounding Diane.

"Can you come over right away? I need to talk to you."

Driving over, Susan was in a panic. What could she have missed? Her knuckles were white on the steering wheel and her breath came in gulps. She forced herself to go carefully and took several deep breaths in the car before going to her sister's door, where a red-eyed Diane met her.

"I felt it was time to tackle that old tin box of Tom's. He kept his old diaries in it. I can't believe what I found. Do you know he had been meeting someone else for over a year before his accident?"

Susan turned white and clutched the arm of the chair before sinking into it.

"Yes, I can see you're shocked. Who would have thought it of him? I was crying for hours last night but now I am just so blazing angry." Diane's voice was rising as she spoke.

By now totally numb, Susan was unable to reply.

"It's all in here," went on Diane, waving a small black book. "All the meetings with someone called Pookie."

MISS ABERCROMBIE'S CAT

Helen Taylor

When the cardboard box arrived, Caro knelt beside it, fingering the string and the lumps of sealing wax at its knots. She recognised the precise copperplate script that had written her name and address, but refused to reveal the contents until Uncle George, handing her the scissors and closing the door gently, left her alone.

It felt as though she had known Miss Abercrombie for a long time, though now she realised it had only been one summer. Caro had arrived in Dundee like an early summer storm, disordering her aunt and uncle's home. Not that she was aware of this. Slump-shouldered and empty-eyed, she looked as desolate as she felt. Initially, she was oblivious to the way the family tiptoed around her. In fact, she was oblivious to everything except her misery. Sometimes she overheard whispered conversations:
"She never smiles. She hardly responds to anything. She's polite enough, I grant you, but it's as if she isn't really here."
"And are you surprised?"
"She hasn't even cried, not once. I'm very worried about her."
"Just give her time."
Gradually she realised how much she could use it to her advantage. Nobody really wanted to tell her off about anything in case it upset her. And so she was able to do as she wished, even if that was to remain frozen in grief and to resist any attempts to draw her out of it. She spent a great deal of time in the garden, enjoying the escape from her younger cousins, tantalised by the view of the laden raspberry canes swaying in the breeze. She worked out a way of climbing the wall and was sitting on it when she first met Miss Abercrombie.
"What on earth are you doing, girl!"
The clipped accents had come from below her on the other side of the wall and Caro almost fell off in surprise at the suddenness.

MISS ABERCROMBIE'S CAT

Through the leaves of the canes, she could only see a slim, upright figure, clad in a dark coat. Pinned to the lapel was a brooch, a silver feather encrusted with stones like diamonds that caught her attention, sparkling in the sunlight. As she approached, Caro could see the fine silver hair and eyes of such a light grey that they looked like pools of mercury, set in ashen skin. The mouth was pale, pursed and angry. Caro had to swallow the last of the raspberries before she could speak, rubbing her berry-stained hands on her jeans nervously.

"I'm so sorry," her voice quavered, "I've been watching your berries for days now and only the birds were eating them. It seemed such a waste…"

"So you thought you'd help yourself. I see. You must be the niece who's come to stay with Dr Mackenzie."

Caro waited for the inevitable softening of the eyes as the old lady recalled the circumstances of her coming to Broughty Ferry and braced herself for the inevitable gush but there was no remission from the disapproving frown. Caro was disappointed yet curiously relieved at the same time

"I arrived just over two weeks ago."

"Indeed. However, even if you are new to our neighbourhood, that does not excuse trespass – or theft for that matter. Did it ever occur to you that I might be happy for the berries to be left for the birds and small animals that live around my garden?"

Caro shook her head, miserable.

"I'm really sorry. I – I didn't know. I won't do it again, honestly."

Caro felt even more uncomfortable as the quicksilver eyes drilled into her, then relaxed as they lost their intensity.

"Well, as long as you've learned, we'll say no more about it. I should introduce myself. I am Miss Abercrombie. And you are?"

"Caro. Short for Caroline."

"Then I will call you Caroline. I don't approve of diminishing names or people. Well, Caroline, as we're going to be neighbours, I think you should come over the wall and have – a hot chocolate? We'll call your visit a payment for the raspberries."

"Like Beauty for the rose in Beauty and the Beast!" Caro suggested.

"I was thinking more of Persephone and the pomegranate seeds in Hades, personally. But yes, that too. I expect you won't have met many people yet."

"No," Caro tried to keep the wistfulness out of her voice but was aware that she didn't succeed, "and it's ages till I start school here. According to Uncle George, time will fly by till the start of term, but it doesn't feel like it now. And I love my little cousins, but…"

"But it would be better to have other company too."

"That's right. And one of them – Emily I think – drew in all my books."

Caro managed to scrape her knee and elbow jumping into the other garden. She hadn't realised how big the house over the wall was until she entered the hall.

"It's even bigger than Uncle George's!"

"I know. It's a monstrosity, in my opinion. My grandfather was one of the jute barons you've no doubt heard about and had this built to show off to his friends. However, one must not be too critical: because of his money my father was able to indulge in his hobby. He was particularly interested in Ancient Egypt, as you can see."

"Are those real mummies?"

"Real mummy cases, at least. Even father drew the line at adorning a room with desiccated corpses."

Caro was ushered into a room, craning back at the mummy cases stacked at regular intervals around the walls of the entrance hall and was left while Miss Abercrombie made the chocolate. It was a large, sunny room that had a view out over the Tay. Caro knew her aunt would have been admiring the cornicing and marble fireplace, but it was the statue on the hearth that caught Caro's attention. It was a large black stone cat, its eyes painted gold and wearing a gold necklace and earring. She knelt down beside it and stroked the smooth stone. Its upright posture and superior air reminded her of Miss Abercrombie herself and Caro smiled to herself.

"You've met Bastet, I see."

As before, Miss Abercrombie appeared silently, holding a tray with a large chocolate cup and a tiny coffee cup on it.

"Bastet was the guardian of the home in Ancient Egypt. She is interested in all things domestic. Bastet, this is our new neighbour, Caroline, who has come to live with her aunt and uncle. While she's here, she has my permission to come into the garden and eat as many raspberries as she likes – as long as she also comes to say hello."

MISS ABERCROMBIE'S CAT

Miss Abercrombie smiled and turned to Caro. "Bastet is another of father's acquisitions in Egypt and now I can't imagine home without her. She loves to hear about everything that happens in a household. When I was younger, I found that if I told her a problem and listened very carefully, I could hear her advice in my heart. And the advice was always good. She is not the most valuable of my father's acquisitions, but she is the most precious to me."

Caro nodded bemusedly. She noticed that the table on which Miss Abercrombie set her coffee cup was actually a chess board and came over to examine the pieces. They looked Egyptian too. Miss Abercrombie explained.

"I am convinced that the set's a fake, but it's so charming I don't care. It's the Gods of order and creation, Isis, Osiris, Horus, Thoth and Ma'at, ranged against the Gods of death and chaos, Set, Sekhmet, Opet, Ammet and Anubis. This is my favourite, Ma'at, goddess of Truth and Justice, with her symbol of the feather. Whenever Egyptians died, their spirit or ka was weighed in a set of scales with Ma'at's feather. If the ka was heavier than her feather from all their sin, they would be sent to Ammet the destroyer and devoured. If it was lighter, they would be allowed into heaven."

"The feather's just like the brooch you're wearing!"

"Indeed, that's why I wear it. So, do you play chess?"

"A little. Dad was teaching me…"

Caro bowed her head as she remembered. She felt a touch, feather light, on her hair.

"I'm so sorry, Caroline."

There was a long silence.

"Would you like to learn again?"

Caro nodded and the game began.

Thus the pattern of the summer was established. Caro would climb over the wall and meet Miss Abercrombie. They would have coffee or chocolate and then they would settle down to their chess. At first, Caro insisted that Miss Abercrombie wielded the gods of order and creation and kept the gods of death and chaos for herself. As she explained, it meant that the good side would always win. However after a few weeks, Miss Abercrombie equally insisted that they alternated sides: a benchmark of Caro's improvement, which hugely pleased her.

Helen Taylor

The old lady often talked wistfully about her childhood in Egypt, of sailing the Nile in a dahabeeyah, of the sites she had been taken to by her father in search of antiquities. "All sun and dust after the relative coolness of the river. No wonder the ancients worshipped them, the river and the sun."

Miss Abercrombie picked up Ma'at and moved her into position. "Check. I had an ayah to look after me during the day as Mother died when I was born. Father turned all his attention to his grand collection of Ancient Egyptian artefacts. A way of coping with his grief, I think. But sometimes in the evenings, he would teach me chess – with this set too… He hardly noticed the mosquito bite at first and soon after it became infected, it was too late. No antibiotics back then… It was the worst journey of my life, sailing home on my own, with only Bastet for company. And Dundee was so cold and lonely. Grandfather did his best, but it can't have been easy for him either…"

Caro imagined a young Miss Abercrombie left to roam in the mansion filled with her father's collection, just as isolated as she had been in Egypt, with a stone cat her only confidant. Seeing no further moves, she toppled Set the slayer on the onyx board.

Miss Abercrombie allowed Caro free range of the house. She loved it: it was full of so many relics from Egypt – from the mummies in the hall to the canopic jars that filled a bedroom and cases of gold and faience jewellery in the library, and she also appreciated the implicit trust. If she had any questions, Miss Abercrombie would always try to answer them, but she said her old bones needed a rest after a strenuous chess game and would allow her the fun of exploring on her own. There was one portrait that fascinated her, of a striking lady wearing an amethyst brooch, standing next to an old-fashioned car. When Caro asked about her, Miss Abercrombie sighed gently.

"That is my grandfather's cousin Elizabeth. That makes her my first cousin twice removed. It was she who inspired my father to visit Egypt in the first place. I'm never sure whether to curse her or be grateful to her."

One day, she was about to walk in to Miss Abercrombie, but she heard a voice speaking and paused to listen, more so that she could tell if she wanted to join Miss Abercrombie and her putative guest or continue her game.

MISS ABERCROMBIE'S CAT

"I know, but she's still so young and sad."

A pause.

"You are, as ever, correct. She is no younger or sadder than I was, I suppose."

A sigh.

Caro crept back up the hall and then charged back to the door noisily. When she came in, only Miss Abercrombie was there. And Bastet by the hearth.

Eventually, the summer passed and Caro went to visit, not over the wall but through the front gate, to show Miss Abercrombie her school uniform. Miss Abercrombie ushered her in and made appreciative noises about her new appearance.

"Actually, Caroline, I've been meaning to talk to you."

Caro had a sinking feeling. When an adult wanted to talk, it invariably meant something bad had happened. She waited in silence.

"Caroline, I have to leave. Now, before it's too late. I've procrastinated too long because I enjoy your company so much. Talking to you about my childhood has made me realise how much I want to visit Egypt again. I feel I must see it, the sun, the river and the dust. And I don't think I will be coming back. In a few weeks, you will receive something from me. Accept it and remember everything I have ever said to you. I know all will be well with you."

They had a last game of chess, which Caro won, and a last hot chocolate.

"Farewell, Caroline. Take care and remember."

Caroline snipped open the string and, heart in mouth, opened the box. She lifted out Bastet, cradling her gently, and placing her on the hearth in her bedroom. Suddenly the tears she had long stifled began to flow and, cradling the stone cat in her arms, she wept for her parents, for Miss Abercrombie and also for herself, having to start life again with strangers in a new city.

Also in the crate was the chess board and a box containing each piece. She picked them out, examining them and placing them in their proper place. She moved one piece, as if to start a new game, but could not bear to move the opposing side, not yet anyway. Maybe in a few days... One day, studying the box which had contained the chess pieces, she noticed it was a little too large. She felt the sides of the box and finally touched the representations of feathers on the lid. There was a satisfying click and out swung a tiny drawer. Within lay the feather brooch. Caro clasped it in her hand.

"Thank you. I still miss you… And I do remember."

She began to speak to Bastet, telling her about her days, the triumphs and the disasters, the new friends and the disappointments, hopes and anxieties. Bastet always listened. And often Caro could hear the cat's response, deep in her heart. And Miss Abercrombie was quite right. Bastet's advice was always very good.

WHAT ELIZABETH BAIN DID NEXT

Ann Prescott

"I haven't seen *her* before. Whatever have you done with Ellen?"

Having been divested of his tall hat, coat, and gloves, Captain Charles Bain followed his sister into the sitting room.

Elizabeth was unpinning her hat in front of the over-mantel mirror. "Whatever do you think? Ellen has moved out to be with her sisters in the Perth Road. To be honest the offer was providential. We both knew the stairs were getting beyond her. Mhari does me very well. Besides, Ellen hasn't gone. She's here every day to do the cooking and if she's not now whizzing up Coburg cakes for Master Charles to take back then I'm a Dutchman."

Her brother grinned and intimated that he would be sure to make his way down to the kitchen before they left. "You and Ellen, the pair of you are like the Rock of Gibraltar for us. You don't know how much this get-together with the all the family means to me, Lizzie. I didn't know how we'd pull through these past months, and that's a fact. Indeed at one time Maria and I wondered whether you might move in with us after... Well, no matter. Here we all are, ready to wet the head of Jane's boy. She could be your own daughter, you know; she was such a babe herself when Ma died!"

"I'm so glad you're able to be here. I thought that winding up the affairs in Calcutta would keep you away for several weeks yet."

"It was touch and go whether I would be back but George's records were in excellent order – trust big brother George – and we made fair headway. That last time – would you believe he stayed on deck the full twenty-eight hours? He didn't budge until we'd put in at Port Said. Egypt mesmerised him. So, when the *Hester Eliza* headed into the Canal and I saw the date was the 19th... and for you, his twin..." Charles coughed loudly. "You're a good egg, Sis, and, in short, Maria and I want you to accept this."

With a bit of a struggle he extracted a square, blue, jeweller's box from his waistcoat pocket. Inside the box was a delicate gold brooch fashioned in the shape of a flower. At its centre was a facetted amethyst surrounded by leaves and petals of green stones and seed pearls.

As Elizabeth struggled with her voice a commotion in the hall signalled the arrival of the next contingent of the christening party. She managed to stuff away her handkerchief before a trio of boys entered the room.

"Aunt Lizzie, Aunt Lizzie, we're back! Pa, may we go down to the Green to watch the trains. Please Pa. Ma says we may if we're not late for lunch."

Prompted by a nod from Maria, Charles gave his consent and Maria, arm in arm with Elizabeth and Charles, went to the front steps to watch the young Bains down Windsor Street. By now the hansom cab conveying Elizabeth's brother and sister, together with their respective spouses, had drawn up. Alfred assisted William Langlands as they carefully handed down Jane, who was holding a bundle swathed in yards of lace from which poked the furious scarlet face of William James Langlands junior. She said she would take him straight upstairs. Everyone else trooped into the sitting room.

Alfred crossed to the decanters. Caroline immediately positioned herself furthest from the fire in the most uncomfortable chair in the room. The Reverend William Langlands graciously allowed himself to be applauded on the admirable manner in which he had conducted the baptismal service before he too joined the men guarding the hearth. They had embarked on their usual enumeration of the vagaries of the Indian Jute Mills Association. Meanwhile Elizabeth and Maria conversed with Caroline and learnt that her daughters were in good health and their aunts would find them much grown. The ladies were as one in agreeing that the spring flowers had been exceptionally fine.

Mercifully, at this juncture Jane tripped in. She announced to the room in general and William in particular that wee Jamie and Emily were fast asleep at last and nurse was under instruction to alert her the instant either of them awoke. She continued, "May I inspect this famous brooch, Lizzie? Maria has been telling me all about it."

Elizabeth blushed, exclaiming whatever must Maria and Charles think of her? She had forgotten her manners in the bustle of arrivals and had been remiss in thanking them.

Jane took it upon herself to fasten the brooch on Lizzie's frock but first she displayed it to her sister-in-law. "Look, Caroline. Have you seen any of the new suffragette pieces yet; white for purity, green for hope, and purple for dignity? I believe they are becoming all the rage."

Caroline, the indulged only daughter of a banker, who was wearing a pearl and diamond choker that Elizabeth privately valued at a king's ransom, murmured something inaudible. However, as the sense of Jane's words came to her, Elizabeth's hand flew to her mouth. "I am having a morning! I never gave the colours a thought... So I *do* have your approbation! Oh, Maria! Charles! Thank you, thank you!"

"And you such a militant too," teased her brother.

William Langlands opined that, although his wife was *pure* in heart and did not lack *dignity*, nevertheless he *hoped* that she would not be tempted to emulate the exploits of the suffragettes.

"Just so," said Alfred unexpectedly.

"One little suffragette sitting in the sun,

By came a bachelor and then there were none."

Jane opened fire. "William, you said that *Mrs* Pethick Lawrence and *Mrs* Despard spoke a great deal of sense, you know you did. And they are positively renowned for their dignity and decorum. And, Alfred, Lizzie has never lacked for beaux!"

"I wasn't referring to Lizzie."

"To whom then, pray?"

If Alfred made a response his voice was lost as Charles added some fuel. "Lizzie's beaux? Remember that lawyer-fellow, Alfred? The one we wagered would build himself a willow cabin on the Green? And now Maria tells me Jane spotted Lizzie with..."

With the ease of long practice Maria shushed her husband and quelled the combatants. She, too, had read the article in the *Advertiser* from which, she assumed, Alfred was quoting. The suffragists' march through the streets of Edinburgh had taken place on the day the Prime Minister launched his campaign against class distinction and class privileges. That it did not include the right of women, both married and single, to vote was provocation enough. In her view the 300 or so women of Dundee who had the courage to stand up against such injustice behaved with admirable restraint. She was proud that Lizzie was counted amongst them. In the silence that followed Elizabeth rang for luncheon.

For the second time that morning Elizabeth's nephews entered the sitting room in a state of high excitement. The middle one fastened on to his father's sleeve like a leech and begged him to look, only look! Charles allowed himself to be tugged to the window... His "By Jove!" brought the others across. Standing at the front door was a dark blue autocar with yellow wheel trims and a side entrance.

"I thought you'd be surprised," said Elizabeth, a shade complacently.

"Is it yours Aunt Lizzie? Ma, Aunt Lizzie says it's hers."

"Does it go?"

"May I sit in it?"

Elizabeth said that it certainly hadn't dropped from the skies and did indeed go.

"Boys!" admonished Maria.

The gentlemen were equally pressing with their questions and harder to subdue. Elizabeth informed them that the autocar was an 18/14 hp Singer. She had considered purchasing a Siddeley, as that was the make the Queen favoured, also Mr Shaw drove one.

"Thomas Shaw, Motor Agent, top of Reform Street, TS 311; two seater body painted grey with red lines," interpolated her eldest nephew. His mother gave him a look.

Elizabeth continued, "When he visited the Motor Show at Olympia November last, Mr Shaw was so impressed by the Singers that he recommended an 18/14 hp version to Miss Eliza Gilroy. She had a green two-seater body built. TS 304," she added with an amused glance at her nephew.

"I thought the Gilroys drove a dark green landaulette," Alfred objected.

"TS 11, White steam car, belongs to Tayworks," piped up the irrepressible mine of information.

"Go on, Lizzie," said Charles, frowning at his son.

"There's not much more to tell. Miss Gilroy was kind enough to take me up for a run. She said that the new live cable transmission was a decided improvement on a chain drive. The chassis was suitable for a double phaeton too, and I thought that that would serve me better than a two-seater."

Jane had taken the opportunity to slip upstairs and peep in on the children. She now returned with Mhari who announced in her soft Highland voice that Ellen had asked her please to inform Miss Bain that

WHAT ELIZABETH BAIN DID NEXT

luncheon was waiting for them in the dining room.

Whilst the children whooped down to the kitchen, the adults seated themselves round the table which had been handsomely set with fresh flowers and the best napery. Elizabeth had opted to serve Aberdeen roll with a vegetable charlotte and green salad accompaniments to be followed by a batter and gooseberry pudding.

After everyone had been helped to a plate, the conversation reverted to the subject of automobilism. The ladies concurred with Jane's dictum that the sack coat was indeed suitable for motoring and stylish to boot, and Caroline volunteered the information that, in their Spring fashions, D.M. Brown's had stocked models in musquash and electric seal that were quite divine.

Maria wanted to know what had prompted Lizzie to purchase a motor car. Elizabeth supposed the notion had come to her at the suffragists' march. She couldn't then resist re-living the thrill of the assembly in King's Park under the scrutiny of the hundreds of spectators perched on Arthur's Seat. The procession had taken an age to form. Mrs Despard, Miss Pankhurst, Mrs Billington-Greig, and someone she didn't recognise, led in a two-horse carriage. The marchers lined up behind their banners; the majority were on foot of course, though some women rode in carriages and there were at least two four-horse charabancs, but what had captured Elizabeth's imagination were the autocars, which, with a sly glance at her brothers, she categorised as "bang up to the minute!"

"But admiring them is one thing, purchasing such a vehicle is quite another," objected Maria.

The men were savouring Ellen's cooking in silence. William looked up. "Were the women actually driving the vehicles, Elizabeth?"

"One or two of the ladies were."

He gave Jane one of his rare smiles. "Don't worry, my love. I am not going to blot my copy book again. I'm angling for a ride!"

Elizabeth was still pondering her response to Maria's question. She said that today of all days she believed she had a lot in common with baby James as she, also, was making a new start! If George had still been alive she doubted whether automobilism would have entered her head…

"And now, I must admit, I've discovered I possess an unexpected aptitude for mechanics!" she concluded.

"Do you mean to drive, yourself, then?" pursued William.

"I have driven on several occasions; Charles dropped it off this morning though. He won't let me try my hand at cornering yet."

Her brother, catching the first part of her response, said that men had far more to fear from Lizzie behind a steering wheel than they did from giving her the vote. However, as she finished talking, and eyes turned towards him, the import of the rest of her speech dawned. He shook his head in mock horror. "Not guilty!"

Jane said, "Charles, *Charles*, Charles Judd! Lizzie?"

CUTTING LOOSE

Mary Davidson

Jousef and Samir hung about outside their little shelter in the backyard of the staff houses of the Jubilee Jute Mill, about two miles north of Khulna. The raised voices from within the house warned them not to venture in, even though by then they should have been preparing the evening meal.

"Don't be ridiculous, Jen. I can't agree to you going off to Calcutta on your own."

"Why not? What do you suppose I'd be doing? Don't you trust me out of your sight for a few days? It's the 1950s, Mark, not the 1850s." Subconsciously Jennifer reached to touch the brooch, bequeathed to her by a suffragette great-aunt, which she'd pinned to her blouse that morning.

"It's not a case of not trusting you. It's just not proper for a young lady to travel alone. It's just not safe."

"Rubbish," replied Jennifer. "Sylvia from the Paper Mill goes about alone all the time."

"I don't doubt that – and neglects that young daughter of hers from what I hear. Those American women are bold enough but I don't want you travelling alone."

Jennifer herself had reservations about the way in which Sylvia so readily appeared to leave Meg in the care of her ayah but she told herself that was none of her business and she couldn't let this chance slip.

"What if Sylvia and I went together?" she said quickly. "Surely you can't object to that? I need a break. I get so depressed in this dead-end place."

"I'll think about it." Mark had clearly run out of arguments and so, with victory within her reach, Jennifer resumed her Memsahib role, marched out to the back door and called to the cook and bearer who scurried back in to prepare dinner.

Mary Davidson

Next morning when Jennifer visited the Paper Mill, Sylvia greeted her enthusiastically and agreed that they should travel together.

"Your Mark sounds like a bit of a stuffed shirt but we can soon sort him out," she declared.

Jennifer felt slightly annoyed at this remark but she knew Americans tended to be rather outspoken so she said nothing. She was much more intent on planning her trip.

Changing the subject, she said, "I've been reading up about Calcutta. I think I'd like to see a polo match on the Maidan and learn more about the culture."

"I don't intend to do much of that sort of thing," Sylvia said. "What we need to do is enjoy ourselves. I know all the best places and I've contacts there. Don't worry. We'll have a ball. Why don't you and Mark come to our social club on Saturday evening? John will soon set Mark straight about the trip."

The two couples met as arranged. Sylvia, with John, her friendly good-looking husband, had clearly made an effort to charm. Her straight shoulder-length hair was bound up in a chingnon and she wore an elegant but modest dress which complimented her slim figure.

As soon as drinks were served and the usual pleasantries over, Mark came straight to the point. "What do you think of the girls going off on their own, John?"

"Oh, no bother. Sylvia is a great traveller. They'll be quite safe. I'll make the travel and accommodation arrangements. It'll give us a chance to get to know one another and maybe fit in some snooker and a game of cards."

A week later the girls were off. Sylvia's smart case held cool day dresses, evening wear and clothes for leisure activities as well as jewellery and make-up. "Just you pack the same as me," Sylvia had instructed. For a second Jen thought of saying that she could pack her own case then decided she was being silly. After all, Sylvia knew the city and she didn't. John himself drove them to the border with India which reassured Mark.

Jennifer was fascinated by everything she saw. For long stretches the road seemed hemmed in by jungle vegetation, a huge tangle of bushes and some taller, thin trees, each reaching up to the light and vying for space with those around. She could pick out stands of bamboo and as the jungle thinned near small villages she saw date palms, coconut palms and banana bushes. Then as they approached a cluster of houses made of split bamboo with banana leaf roofs, they saw women outdoors cooking over fires of dried cow dung.

Sylvia, who had been intent on polishing her nails, now screamed at John. "Shut the windows! That smell is vile. Why do they use that stuff for fuel?"

"Because it's free," John replied calmly, "and there's not enough wood nearby that's suitable for burning."

Jennifer was taken aback by Sylvia's outburst. Why should she be upset by something so trivial?

At the border, the guard eyed them disapprovingly. "Are you ladies travelling unaccompanied?"

Sylvia responded defiantly. "We have each other. My husband drove us here and a car is waiting for us at the other side to take us directly to the Great Eastern Hotel in Calcutta."

No further questions were asked, though their passports were carefully scrutinised before the girls were allowed to pass. Jennifer breathed a sigh of relief. Sylvia's outspokenness could, it seemed, have its uses.

As arranged, a car awaited them. Jennifer was amazed at the contrasts on the way. The country roads, like those in East Pakistan, were made of crushed red brick. The villages they passed through were draped with cheap colourful paper banners heralding the start of Divali or the Festival of Lights, a five day celebration of the return of the Hindu deity Lord Ra and his wife Sita to India after his defeat of the demon king of Sri Lanka. Village women had made small clay lamps filled with oil. Jennifer asked the driver about them.

"They will be lit around the houses each year during Divali. This time in early November is also the start of the New Year when it is said the Lakshmi, goddess of good fortune, visits every house lit by a lamp. "

Jennifer listened attentively to the explanation and couldn't understand why Sylvia appeared to be watching her with wry amusement.

The road often passed directly through a village. Wandering goats scattered as the car went past and hens which had been rooting for insects around the roadside suddenly took off in a flurry, shedding feathers like confetti over the car. Apart from the produce of their animals, the villagers appeared to exist on vegetables grown around their houses and whatever they could gather from nearby jungle. They looked poor and workworn.

Roads improved as the car neared the city, the outskirts of which went on for miles, gradually becoming more built up. As they approached the centre the buildings became noticeably more European in style – the remains of the British Raj, Jennifer thought, though these and the modern office blocks and large churches, vied for place with the highly decorated temples. In contrast many streets consisted mainly of open-fronted shops which served also as the dwellings of the vendors. At street corners there were market stalls selling fruit and vegetables. Everywhere people and more people were on the move – workmen, beggars, women with children and rickshaw wallahs, manouevering between cars, lorries and carts of all kinds. Amongst them all, cows wandered freely apparently unfazed by the constant blaring of car horns.

Jennifer began to feel afraid. "How on earth will we get through here?" she asked Sylvia who merely shrugged.

The driver laughed. "We will get there safely. Do not worry. It just takes a little longer than out on the open road."

Sure enough he soon delivered them safely to the Great Eastern Hotel.

Next morning Jennifer was looking forward to exploring the city but first there was breakfast when she was as keen as Sylvia to choose foods such as bacon, pork, sausages, kippers, prunes or even porridge – all things which were unavailable in their part of East Pakistan.

"Right," Sylvia said when they had eaten their fill. "The tennis club first, I think, and then maybe a bit of swimming. They're member only, of course, but luckily my friends can sign us in."

And so the pattern for the mornings was established. Jennifer couldn't help noticing that these clubs Sylvia favoured, though open to all, were mainly patronised by ex-Pats as were the air-conditioned coffee shops and restaurants Sylvia always chose as a cool retreat from the hot afternoon sunshine. Firpo's, famous for its ice cream and cakes, was a particular favourite. So she was cheered on their third morning when Sylvia suggested they do some shopping at the large indoor market.

CUTTING LOOSE

Alighting from their rickshaw at the entrance to the market, they were immediately met by young boys eager to carry their purchases while inside they were assailed on all sides by traders anxious for them to examine their goods. Despite the protestations they quickly passed the fresh meat stalls where other young boys were kept busy shaking flies from the hanging carcasses. Next came the live animal area where they saw monkeys, parrots, mynah birds, small multi-coloured song birds and a mongoose in a variety of cages, while a snake lay curled up in a basket. Jennifer might have stopped to sample the variety of fruits and sweetmeats on sale but Sylvia had other ideas. She was intent on what she called 'real shopping' and bought crocodile shoes and matching handbag while Jennifer settled for a brooch and bracelet of filigree silver.

Next Sylvia insisted they should each buy dress lengths and with the fabric chosen, she arranged for it to be made up in their chosen styles by a local tailor and delivered to them within thirty-six hours. "Beats New York or London prices," she laughed. The sun was setting as they went by taxi back to the hotel. On their way, Jennifer noticed the many Divali lights lit in and around the houses.

"Perhaps," she suggested, "we might visit a Hindu Temple tomorrow?" but Sylvia was quick to scoff at this idea.

"What a quaint little thing you are," she chided. "I've saved something really special for tomorrow."

The 'something special' turned out to be a walk down Chiteranjan Avenue, a broad thoroughfare in a smart area. Here shops had proper glass windows with displays of expensive jewellery. As they arrived at the front of one particularly exclusive looking emporium, Sylvia said, "Let's go in."

They were greeted politely and shown complete sets of jewellery set in gold with rubies, emeralds, diamonds and other precious stones. There were also necklaces, earrings, nose rings, arm and ankle bangles – all well outside their price range. Nevertheless Sylvia began to try on rings and necklaces, preening herself in a long mirror. Having finished with one collection, she moved on to the next.

Jennifer could see that the shopkeeper was becoming restless and she herself was feeling more and more embarrassed. Finally, the shopkeeper asked, "Beg pardon, lady, but do you intend to buy?"

"No, I'm just looking. They're beautiful, of course, but not to my taste," Sylvia said dismissively.

"Sorry," Jen murmured.

"What on earth are you apologising to him for?" Sylvia demanded even before they were safely out of the shop.

"You have no idea, do you?" Jennifer responded angrily. Hailing a passing taxi, she got in, leaving Sylvia staring open-mouthed on the pavement.

Now thoroughly fired up, Jennifer asked the driver to take her to the small temple she had seen close to the hotel. Inside it seemed dark at first but here also were many Divali lights. Larger oil lamps illuminated a wall depicting scenes from the Ramayana, an epic poem telling the story of Lord Rama's many exploits. There were also several statues round the walls and Jennifer was pleased to be able to recognise those of Rama and his wife, Sita. A few worshippers prayed in front of them and laid offerings of fruit and flowers at their feet. The sun was low in the sky when she left the temple and travelled back to the hotel in one of the waiting rickshaws.

Sylvia breezed in some time later and in silence changed quickly into an evening dress. Pausing briefly to mention that she'd arranged to meet a friend, she then headed off to the bar. Jennifer could only feel relieved. She was not enjoying this visit as she should have been. Although the heat of the day had begun to fade, she felt like a breath of air and stepped out onto the balcony of their room. Suddenly the sky was ablaze with light. Of course, it was Divali and this was the obligatory firework display. Jen stood entranced as multi-coloured stars shot into the sky accompanied by the occasional bang of a firecracker or the whoosh of a rocket ascending then filling the air with glorious streaks of light as they burst over the watching crowd below. This sea of colour and the strange exotic costumes were the India she had come to see.

Suddenly John's voice came back to her. "Sylvia's a great traveller." Jennifer almost laughed out loud. Yes, Sylvia liked to notch up the names of the places she'd visited but she carried her own narrow view of the world with her wherever she went.

That was when she realised that she herself could no longer be content with her previous life of tea parties, badminton matches or mah-jong afternoons. Yes, some of these activities were linked to

CUTTING LOOSE

fund-raising to allow poor children in the district go to school but, she realised, she wanted much more active involvement and as soon as she returned home, she'd find ways of being of use. She found herself looking forward to the shocked look on Sylvia's face when she told her of her decision.

PICKY

Deborah Williams-Kurz

On the way out of her Psychology class, Meg happened to glance over at the couple who had sat next to her as they walked out of the fluorescent-lit room. The girl convulsed with a mock shiver as her boyfriend nodded emphatically. Meg moved in closer to hear a snippet of their conversation.

"Her picking freaks me out!" the red headed girl was saying. "If it's not the skin on her fingers then it's her arm hairs. Gross!"

Meg knew, absolutely, that they were talking about her. And the worst part was that they were right. She spent hours making sure her lip liner was perfect, her hair shiny and bouncy like a magazine ad, her breath freshened with the strongest of mints. Yet she never noticed how her primping had slipped out of her private world and into the public arena. In fact every time she left the house she carefully checked her nose hairs for unwanted visitors. Meg would never pick her nose in public. Not even in the car. So how had this penchant for picking escaped her notice?

Immediately she vowed to end it – in public at least. She headed to the overcrowded campus store and purchased a small plastic-covered journal in which to document all plucks, prods and picks. The campaign towards self-improvement had begun.

While sitting on a wooden bench near her next class, Meg took a moment to organize her journal. She used a ruler to create columns for date and time, location and type of behaviour. As she ruminated on the next step, Meg noticed she had been absentmindedly plucking her eyebrows, holding the hairs firmly between thumb and forefinger, and brushing them against her upper lip.

"Stop!"

She noted the action carefully in her book.

Meg decided to skip the rest of her classes for the day. Surely focusing energy on bettering herself was top priority.

PICKY

Her apartment was calm. She had taken on a part-time job, supplementing her university grant, in order to have the luxury of living alone. Meg sat down on the pillowed couch and stared at her hands. She thought about her childhood nail biting. It had got so bad that the ragged remnants of her fingernails would bleed, the tender raw flesh exposed. Her exasperated father simply couldn't understand.

"A nice looking, well-groomed set of hands is one of the main physical traits a man looks for in a woman. Don't you want to be attractive?" he had asked. He hadn't added, "Like your mother," but Meg knew he was thinking it.

Of course she'd wanted to be attractive. What twelve-year old girl didn't? But she could not stop, no matter how much bitter tasting liquid he swabbed on her stinging fingers. Finally, it was the fake fingernails that had done the trick. Meg was completely obsessed with keeping the lacquer perfect. Any sign of a chip would send her into a nail painting frenzy. She glanced down at her perfect French manicure with a sense of pride.

It was time to be pro-active. She knew just what to do. Meg pulled down her beauty kit from above the medicine cabinet in the bathroom and removed the key ingredients. A simple wax treatment and her gold-tipped tweezers were all she needed.

Meg began with the eyebrows. Once removed they could no longer cause trouble and she could create any type of arch she wanted with her eyeliner pencil. She didn't mind the quick bite of the tweezers as they freed each hair from its follicle. On she continued until her eyes merged with her forehead with no fuzzy impediment in between. Next, she heated the wax to use on her arm hair. A smooth arm would look so much more feminine. Meg would be streamlined, like a swimmer.

Half-way through, Meg realized that she had grossly underestimated the amount of wax she needed to complete the process. She couldn't possibly leave the house to go buy more wax with one arm sleek and the other furry like an ape, so she attacked her right arm with the tweezers in order to finish the job. Meg was sure that the look would be phenomenal after the swelling went down.

Now though she needed more time to finish her beautification, so she psyched herself up to call in sick for work. After practicing her raspy voice and her fake baritone cough, Meg quickly picked up the phone and made the call before she could talk herself out of it.

Afterwards, she stood in front of her full-length mirror and assessed her naked body. There was a lot of work to be done, but she had all night.

She couldn't wait to see the red headed girl's reaction in the morning. By the time Meg was done, no one would ever make fun of her again.

No-one.

Story Wheel Five

THE DISC JOCKEY

Nan Rice

It was referred to grandly as 'The Studio' but the new radio station, situated at the rear of a half empty furniture store, was little more spacious than a walk-in cupboard and barely able to accommodate the necessary equipment and two operatives.

A young DJ and technician were seated alongside each other at the work surface. The DJ flicked a bead of sweat from his forehead with his left index finger whilst groping in his trouser pocket with his right hand. Good, he had a handkerchief. He quickly mopped his brow and took a deep breath. Either there was insufficient air circulating in the studio or he'd had a quick rush of adrenalin. The red light flashed in front of him indicating that the moment had arrived. He leaned closer to the mike.

"Good evening, all you Nightingales out there. Let me introduce myself. I'm Wayne Golightly, your new 'Hour Before Midnight' DJ. And that's exactly what I hope to do with the music until the midnight hour. Go lightly." The pseudo American tones of the deep south drifted gently over the airwaves as his first ever live broadcast sprang to life. "While I gradually calm you down, *you* can speak gently to *me*. You're only a 'phone call away, so let's hear from you. I'm going to begin with something really romantic to lull you into mellow mood."

He pressed the green button. Loud samba music reverberated around the studio. "Aye, aye, aye, aye, aye, I like you vee…rrrry much." He almost fell off his seat. It was the wrong record. It wasn't the one he'd put in first this afternoon. In fact he hadn't selected it at all. Some funny bugger had done for him. Wayne mopped his brow again. Should he stop it? If he did, what would he say? No. Best just let it run and say something funny when it finishes.

He gestured to the pallid, spotty face with the mop of long bright red hair sitting adjacent to him with a smirk on his face.

"Charlie, check the next one."

THE DISC JOCKEY

The reply was immediate. "You're So Beautiful."

Thank God. That should have been the first. The hanky came into play again and he sat taking deep breaths. In and out. In and out. The record lasted an eternity.

"Hi again, Nightingales. Just kidding there." The accent slipped somewhat as he struggled for words. "That was literally a blast from the past. Wanted to make sure you are indeed listening to me. That was a famous film actress from the 1940's. The radio told us last week she had died. Sad, but thar ya go. Heigh ho off we go again."

As the music started he glared hatred at Charlie. That bastard had changed the record. He leaned back in his chair to relax before the next record, and think of himself, as was his wont. Nineteen years of age, six feet tall, good looking, loving life, and making good progress in his chosen career. His next move would be to the big one. Radio Tay. He glanced at his reflection in the window opposite and ran his hand lightly over his brown carefully highlighted hair, while allowing the gentle melody of 'You're So Beautiful' to engulf him.

As it reached its conclusion he sat upright. "Oh, oh. My first caller is on the line. Good evening, Nightingale. Come in, come in. Speak to Wayne."

"Hi Wayne. Eh'm Michelle." Was the Dundee voice slightly slurred?

"Hi Michelle," he made an attempt to bury the rude awakening he had inflicted. "How did you like Carmen?"

"Wha?"

"Carmen Miranda."

"Never heard o er."

"Well, Michelle, you're probably too young to know her. Only heard of her last week myself. Can I be impolite and ask your age?"

"Eh'm seventeen, Wayne. Eh've goat a problem."

"I love helping people with problems. Let's have it."

"Eh'm goin' tae jump aff the Tay Bridge when ye've finished yer program, but Eh dinna ken whether t' mak it the Dundee side or the Fife side or maybe right in the middle."

"Well," Wayne thought briefly, "where are you now?"

"Eh'm on the Dundee side."

"Then take the Dundee side, unless maybe you feel like a wee walk. I think the bridge is supposed to be a mile or something long."

"Eh dinna mind walkin', Wayne, but Eh wunnered aboot the tides."

"Sorry, Michelle, now you've got me. I don't know if the tide's up or down. Does it matter all that much?"

"Eh ken there's loadsa big humps o' sand sometimes. E've seen 'em."

"Now *that* could be a problem, Michelle. I know where you're coming from. You could break a leg if you landed on one, and a bonnie wee lass like you wouldn't want that. Maybe you should phone the Coastguard, they'll know whether the tide's up or down."

"Ta, Wayne, Eh'll dae that. Thanks for your help. 'night."

"Goodnightingale." He heaved a sigh of relief. Well that went alright. He was doing fine. His star was rising. His ambition was to be like Ward McGaughrin on Radio Tay. Now there *was* a Top Man. Wayne got through the rest of his shift without further mishaps, or phone calls.

As Wayne put on his anorak Charlie said, "A daft woman called Jessie keeps phoning here looking for a DJ called Hughie something. Won't believe he's not here. If she 'phones again I'm going to tell her to try the loony bin."

Wayne left without replying. He hoped the bright yellow plooks on Charlie's face and neck would get bigger and bigger until they outgrew his nose.

As soon as he reached his flat he dived for the phone and, after dialling, had to wait several minutes.

"Hello. Who's calling please?" The voice was mature but alert.

"Auntie Jessie. It's me. Why did you keep calling the radio station tonight? You shouldn't phone me when I'm working."

"Hughie. You workin'! Eh pit the radio on tae hear ye but it was some daft gowk called Wayne something wi' a yankee accent. Where wir ye? Eh wis worrit aboot ye. Eh phoned four times but naebody kent ye."

"Auntie Jessie, *that was me*. Wayne Golightly's my stage name."

"What's wrang wi' Hughie McWhirter?" Auntie Jessie, agitated, was shouting loudly. "That's yer name."

"I'm tired." The show had been more demanding than Hughie could have imagined. "Is that what you were 'phoning me about?" He could visualise the short rotund person with the mop of grey hair bouncing up and down in annoyance.

"No. Mind Eh telt ye Grace across the landin hud tak no weel

THE DISC JOCKEY

a few weeks ago an wis taen tae the infirmary? Well the doctor there pit her intae a nursing hame 'cos noo she'll no manage on er ain. Mind you, wan day she bought a big tub o chocolate ice cream then couldnae remember whar she pit it. The cleaner fund it three days later when she wis hoovering alow the bed. Anyhow when eh went to see Grace Eh telt the matron aboot how good you were at bein a DJ an that, and she ast if ye could dae a turn at the nursing hame?"

Hughie, whose usually laid back manner was becoming frayed, perked up. "That's great, Auntie Jessie," he said, agog with excitement. "When do they want me?"

"The morn. Three 'til four."

"An hour. Great. How much are they going to pay me?"

"Money wisnae mentioned. I think it's apposed to be a charity do."

"You're joking. I'm a professional. Professionals get paid in hard dosh."

"Hughie, Jimmy Saville did a lot for charity. His hand was never oot his pocket."

"I could put my hand in my pocket too, but it would come out empty." Hughie was torn between delight at the prospect of his first ever gig, and disappointment that it was a poor do. "OK, Auntie Jessie. I'll do it. But it's too soon in my career to be doing freebies. Next time anybody asks about me, talk readies. OK?"

"That's great. The folks'll luv ye." She chose to ignore the subject of payment. "Pick me up the morra at half past twa and Eh'll tak ye there?"

At 2.30 p.m. next day Hughie rammed his finger onto the doorbell and kept it there. He had to, to make sure Auntie Jessie heard it. Then she had to lumber her huge weight down the hall to the door. Eventually he heard keys being turned and bolts withdrawn. Finally the door opened about three inches.

"Wha's there?" Jessie's face peered at him through the opening.

"Auntie Jessie, it's me. It's Hughie. You know it's me. You can see me."

"Eh've goat tae ask cos eh've goat tae mak sure. *The Tully* ayways says no' tae let onybody in."

"Auntie Jessie, I'm not *onybody*. I'm Hughie, your nephew. Open the door."

"OK, well then. Haud oan a meenit." The door was banged shut and he heard the security bolt being scraped from its rest.

He could never understand why, when she could see him quite clearly, she had to ask, 'who's there'? Did you go a bit wonky or something when you got old? Maybe he should knock himself off before he was forty. Do something dramatic like, 'Famous DJ, Wayne Golightly, attempts to hold back moving train with his bare hands – for charity'. Great publicity stunt. Over and above everything else Auntie Jessie obviously hadn't been out this morning.

The door opened and five feet high by five feet wide Auntie Jessie stood there smiling.

"Hello, Hughie, this is awfy guid o' ye." She stood aside and at last Hughie got into the house.

"I thought you went for your messages in the morning? Are you not feeling well?"

"Eh've bin fur meh messages. Eh goat sausages fur meh tea."

"Then why's the door all locked up?"

"Eh loacked it when Eh came back just in case sumdy manages tae get intae the buildin. Wi Grace being awa an er hoose across there bein empty Ehm here m'sel an the twa doonstairs widnae hear if Eh yelled fur help."

"Have you heard how Grace is doing?"

"It's terrible, Hughie. That night she took bad it wis wi' a stroke an a heart attack at the wan time. Noo she's no able tae manage. It's no fair, Hughie, because that hoose next door is a palace. Hiv ye been in it?"

Hughie shook his head.

"Her nephew wiz up yesterday an said he'd tae empty it and sell it aff. Aa her lovely stuff goin God knows where an her in a hame." Jessie fished a pure white handkerchief from her cardigan pocket and rubbed it across her eyes.

Hughie had never seen his auntie upset before. "Auntie Jessie, get your coat and shoes on, and we'll go and see Grace."

Jessie immediately went to the bedroom and returned wearing her best coat and shoes. "Hiv ye goat yer record player wi ye, Hughie?"

"It's a compact disc player, Auntie Jessie. Record players are old-fashioned. I'm saving up to buy the proper gear, but this'll do for now. Let's go."

THE DISC JOCKEY

When they reached the nursing home the Matron greeted them affably and escorted Hughie to the lounge while Jessie went to visit Grace.

Hughie was surprised at how well furnished and posh the place was. And it smelt nice. He placed his equipment on a small table and watched the residents being led in slowly and helped into comfortable armchairs. An elderly gentleman, leaning heavily on a stick, hobbled up to him.

"I'm eighty-five. Eighty-six on my next birthday. Do you smoke?"

"Sorry. I don't."

"Neither do I. Makes it bloody awkward if somebody asks you for a fag." He hobbled off and edged into an armchair.

Hughie counted twelve occupied chairs when the Matron nodded to him and mouthed. "That's the lot." He looked round in horror. Already some of them were sleeping. If he'd have known this was how it was going to be, he would have suggested that woman from Estuary FM to do the gig.

A tall thin lady arrived and rushed up to him. "I've never seen you before. You're new?"

"I'm a visitor. I'm here with my auntie."

"Well you can take me with you when you go. Can you tell me where the shops are?"

He pointed in the direction of the main door and she rushed off.

Hughie smiled broadly to his audience then, in his stage drawl said, "Good afternoon, ladies and gentlemen, what kind of music would you like to start with? Something slow and romantic, or…"

"The cha cha cha," and the old fellow with the stick catapulted onto the floor, stumbled, returned to his chair and sat down, then closed his eyes.

The tall thin lady returned. "They're shut." She rushed off again.

"OK folks, let's get goin' with the Bee Gees."

'Stayin' Alive' failed to entice anyone to dance. Neither did the following two records. Most of the audience were sleeping. "No wonder they didn't want to pay me," Hughie muttered to himself. What on earth would they be interested in? The next record was Carmen Miranda. "That bloody Charlie's done it in again." His scowl became a smile. These people would remember her.

As soon as the record started the 85-year-old shot off his chair and headed for a small, attractive woman seated near him. "Fancy a dance, doll?"

"Fuck off," she said politely.

He headed for Hughie. "The things I would like to do to her." Don Juan rolled his eyes and growled like a lion. "Excuse me, son. Gotta go to the Little Boy's Room."

At this juncture a Careworker arrived pushing a trolley. Miraculously, twelve pairs of eyes opened expectantly. The girl served Hughie first. He opted for coffee and a cream doughnut from the selection of goodies. He noticed every resident selected two or three cakes, and that all eyes stayed open while the jaws operated. Afternoon tea took almost half an hour. Thereafter some eyelids clattered down again.

Don Juan hobbled into the lounge and shouted from the door, "Hi son, sorry to be so long. Constipated."

Hughie glanced at his watch. Five to go. He started the next record without looking at the title. Why bother, no-one was interested. Once it ended he would be offski.

"Hughie."

Startled, he turned. "Auntie Jessie."

"Grace's no' well. Ah sat wi her an held her haund fur company. Eh miss her." Tears welled in Jessie's eyes.

Hughie sensed her distress. As he lifted his equipment he glanced at his audience and suddenly realised that, once upon a time, they had all been real people.

"Come on, pal. We'll go to Visocchi's for an ice cream." He put his arm around her shoulder and, as they walked towards the door he said loudly, "Bye bye for now, folks. See you next week. Same time, same place."

DIAL EMMA
(for murder)

Ward McGaughrin

I never imagined I'd have too much difficulty. Someone does it every day. The idea's been swimming around my head for ages. Every single stroke is becoming part of the plan. The finishing line is within easy reach. And Morrissey sings.

It has to be done. Thinking in sequence, entry to the building is first. I'd be too obvious trying to disable the CCTV cameras. The view from every one of those nasty little devices includes at least one of the other cameras. Anyway, a 20-foot ladder would look odd on the roof of my Fiat 500, so that's out.

Could I call on Bill our chief engineer? There's been no love lost between that pair ever since the 'pizza and Coke all over the sound desk' incident two years ago. And it was Bill who tipped me off about Marmite Emma – though I've still to find anyone who actually loves her – and my fiancé, Dave. But should I involve him? He could easily create a camera fault which happens on cue. That's a maybe.

Sound desk? Oh… My… God! Yes. Hidden in plain sight. That's all I need, one big empty flight case. Musicians are in and out of here at all hours of the day hiring and returning equipment.

"You want to what?" Johnny stared at me as if I wanted him to put a Spice Girls song into his live set. The legend was he'd been playing bass before he could walk. It might have been true. His four strings owned any live gig or recording they'd ever been part of. He'd been in a dozen bands, but was always best known for The Books. They'd recorded two albums and supported Bryan Adams a few years back, but those 'musical differences' came through again and he now owned and ran the Casablanca recording studios in the Estuary FM complex. "Climb into a flight case like a magician's assistant waiting to be sawn in half?"

"Yeah, that's about it. Do you have one that'd fit?"

"What are you five six, five seven?"

Ward McGaughrin

"About there, but I'm flexible…" I knew by his eyebrows, that was one of those 'I didn't mean to say it like that' moments but he didn't comment. It's just one of his qualities I've always loved…

"That one should do, the big one with The Books stencil. It takes my three Rickenbackers easy. What is it you want to do again?"

"I just want to surprise someone, no big deal." I know he doesn't believe me… I don't even believe me.

"You'll need someone to push you to wherever you're going… and then to let you out. Houdini couldn't escape from inside one of these when they're locked. And you can't be in there for too long, it's just about airtight… you'd suffocate."

I liked the plan less with each word. Plus it's another two or three people to involve. But Morrissey sang louder and spurred me on.

I'm still clinging to this flight case scenario. If I make it inside the building then to all intents and purposes, I'm invisible. Timing is all. It's that 'Sex, love and relationships' phone-in for her first three hours, then it's an hour of blues and soul to end with. 'Dial Emma'. I've always thought it was a naff name for the show, aside from the irony that the bitch managed to hand out advice with honesty and sincerity at the same time as her illicit affair. And all the time they were at it, I was on air, so they'd no fear of me walking in on them… He'd even phone me on the pretence of saying goodnight. But the bosses love the title, the show… and her.

It's got to be that last hour. She puts the songs on autopilot and closes the blinds on the studio windows for… 'recreational reasons'. I have no idea how the place can smell so pristine after her little sessions, but she manages it.

That's the When sorted, just the How to settle on. Thanks Morrissey, although the knot's easy enough, sadly there's no place for a noose.

Strangulation would leave fingerprints or bruising on her neck. Even if I could manage the physical stuff, it would show someone else was in there with her. Self-strangulation is a wee bit far-fetched.

What if she could poison herself. How much would I need? How long would it take? I've no idea, but it's probably somewhere on the net… which would leave some kind of footprint on my computer. So that would be another no, then.

It's just going to have to be one single gunshot. Empty building, soundproof studio... I like the sound of this.

All I need is a gun. "All I need is a gun"? Listen to yourself, girl. Sadly, or maybe, thankfully, easier said than done. There's knowing who to ask. I'd have to ask someone about that... then find the supplier. Hah! That makes it sound like popping into Guns R Us. There's bound to be a pub in this city where I could find one. Maybe near the docks or the bus station. I bet Paul in the newsroom would know. He's in with the bricks and 'knows where the bodies are buried' when it comes to politicians and gangsters. For some reason he always puts them in the same category. I know he could point me in the right direction for the wrong people.

I knew it would be the Zanzi Bar; it's as dark as it is loud. If there'd been a piano player, he'd have stopped. The word 'seedy' was invented for this place. I'm sure there's stuff growing in the carpet; it's like walking on peat.

"Tia Maria and Babycham... with ice." Did I really ask for that? Surely Paul's winding me up. The female behind the bar doesn't bat an eyelid. Her face is familiar... think I've seen her on Mount Rushmore. She's hard. She returns with the glass, a bottle and a four digit number written on a beermat. She gestures to the keypad on the door... I can't do this, I choose the door marked exit.

This is now going to involve another unknown number of shady customers added to Johnny, plus someone to let me out of the flight case. All of a sudden I'm accumulating more experts than Danny Ocean.

Would I have the bottle to use a gun anyway? Probably not, if I'm honest. Maybe I don't have to. What about a hit-man? Wad of cash, clear conscience. Could leave myself open for blackmail though and I'd probably have to go back to that pub again.

I look up hoping for that big cartoon lightbulb to appear. It doesn't, but I'm thinking lightbulb... electricity... shock. That would do it. Right, where's Bill's e-mail about pizza and Coke in the sound desk. I'm sure he goes on about electricity's killing potential.

Really must clear out this in-box. I'll save that joy for another day, though. 'Power outage', no that's not it... 'Coffee cups... no... here it is: 'No food in studio. Blah blah... incident... company rules...

obeyed... mess... damage... All electrical equipment which has a metallic construction has to be earthed. By earthing I mean that there is a cable connected to the metalwork of the unit and this cable is connected to the earth cable of the mains lead. If the live mains makes contact with any of the metalwork, because it is earthed the current flows unrestricted which will blow the fuse hence making the unit safe. If the metalwork was not earthed the metalwork would be live. You touching the metalwork then gives the electrical current a route to earth and the current flowing through will kill you.'

So, it's safe... at the moment. All I need to do is make it unsafe by disconnecting some wire or other... without killing myself in the process. Beads of sweat, pulsing music, snippers in hand, red wire, blue wire, red wire... think I'll switch off that idea.

There must be another way in to let me do this. Where's Jonathan Creek when you need him to solve a locked room problem in reverse? Once the studio door's shut not even sound can get in or out. It's only texts and e-mails which get in and I can't kill her with a mysterious electronic poison pen letter. She lives to breathe another day.

Lightbulb moment again! Breathing. The air conditioning into the studio... the intake thingies are outside. A big hose from my car's exhaust and the thing would just suck the fumes straight into the studio. How long does that take though? You see it on those TV shows where some person's in the garage and they've hooked the hose into the car and closed all the windows. No, they always have intent. All she'd have to do is open the studio door to escape. But what if it was a different gas... something quick and deadly...   something which clears quickly so nobody else is injured?

Another potentially good idea evaporates before my very eyes. Deadly Poisonous Gasses R Us probably isn't worth Googling.

Maybe I should take it down a notch or two from murder. Stink Bombs would be much easier to find. She'll be on air coughing and spluttering and feeling wretched... good enough for now. Tam Shepherd's in Glasgow, that'll do the trick.

"Hi, I wonder if you can help me. Do you have a supply of Stink Bombs in stock?"

"Now that's going back a bit."

"What do you mean?"

DIAL EMMA

"You'd probably be able to find them on the internet somewhere, but we've not had them for a while."

"How long's a while and will you be getting any more in?"

"Sorry, we've not had them for over ten years so we'll not be getting any more in. Anything else I can help you with?"

"No, thanks, that's all I was after."

Well, even that idea's done a vanishing act.

Something tells me I'm giving her too much energy. Revenge is a dish best served cold.

I'll just do nothing except get on with my life – like Joanna, my hypnotherapist pal, says I should. So every day I try to tell myself Emma, the nasty bitch, is welcome to him, the slimy two-timing arrogant creep. He'll probably do the same to her as well and 'vice' versa. They deserve each other.

Drowning, now I hadn't thought of that…

BLESSINGS

J. Stirling

"I send out blessings. From the depths of my soul I send out light and love. With each breath in I dissipate all your anxiety, the injustices, the pain. With each breath out I offer my healing…"

With one long sigh I returned to my earthly body, stretched my limbs and opened my eyes. My Sanctum was a tranquil paradise with its plain white walls, stripped pine floorboards and leafy umbrella plants in large pots. The gentle rhythm of waves lapping on a pebble beach played on the CD. I blew out the rose scented candles and retired to bed with Samson padding at my heels.

The next morning I breakfasted outside underneath the oak tree which I had once thought might hold a tree house and rope swing but instead held fat little sparrows and tinkling wind chimes. The morning was full of promise and I gave thanks for the great beauty of the world. The peacefulness of the garden always nourished my soul with positive energy. Every sparrow, every smooth round pebble, every delicate spider's web was physical evidence that goodness prevailed and I never took them for granted.

With a sense of pleasant anticipation I checked the diary: hypnotherapy for little Caroline who was coping so well with the loss of her parents, my monthly healing session with Louise whose cancer was about to go into remission, Angel Therapy for Tom, who was caring for his elderly mother, and at four pm – Calum. The highlight of my week.

Most people who came to me were initially enthusiastic about embracing meditation as part of their daily life but as time passed they often didn't have the time to keep it up and after a few months they were back where they started. But Calum was different.

A shy man in his early forties, he was devoid of all self-worth. In our initial consultation I learned that he worked full-time as an architect while taking on complete responsibility for his one-year-old twin daughters and managing the family home. Although this was taking its toll on his mental and physical health, he acknowledged that it was his feelings of inadequacy as a husband which had brought him to my door.

His dark eyes glowed as he recounted how he had met Rovena almost two years ago on a walking holiday in the Albanian Alps. It had been a whirlwind romance and they had returned to Scotland as man and wife.

"I love her so much and can only blame myself for her coldness towards me."

"In what way do you feel you are to blame?" I'd prompted.

"Well… if I worked harder I could buy her everything she desires and if I wasn't so hopeless she might want to spend more time with me."

On that day I resolved to do all I could to make the marriage work so that Calum could enjoy the happiness he deserved and through our weekly hypnotherapy sessions Calum *had* learned to value himself, growing in confidence and self-esteem. He was promoted at work and found joy in every aspect of his life, especially his beloved daughters. He had committed to my teachings absolutely but Rovena's affection remained elusive and this continued to trouble him.

When the last of my clients left the Sanctum, I barely had time to change my blouse and straighten my hair before Calum arrived.

On the doorstep he met me with a smile that radiated self-assurance and my heart soared to see how much progress we had made since his first visit. We shared a pot of detox herbal tea while he filled me in on his week.

"I think things are definitely heading in the right direction," he told me. "We had been talking about going on a family holiday a few months ago but had to wait till the twins' passports and Rovena's UK passport came through. When they arrived on Wednesday she seemed really delighted."

"That's wonderful news!" I thrilled.

"Well, I thought she'd be keen to start planning the holiday with me but she's even more distant than usual."

"If you like I could speak to her in my meditations tonight. My blessings might help her recognise what wonderful qualities she has in you. In the meantime I'll include some powerful morale boosting in the hypnotherapy for you."

As I closed the door behind him I noticed the pile of post from the morning. It was all the usual junk mail, all except the large blue envelope bearing the familiar crest of Craigmore Academy. Once a year I received the former pupil's newsletter. I had little interest in reading about the great successes of my former tormentors so took the newsletter up the stairs to file it where it belonged.

    The forty watt bulb hanging from the ceiling barely lit the centre of the attic room. It was here I shut away all the souvenirs of the hurt, the humiliation and the cruelty of my childhood. The newsletters were in a pile next to the fake Valentine's card Pamela Easton had sent me as a joke. Next to them lay my teenage diary, a bottle of perfume I had worn only once and a pile of letters I had written to my mother but never sent. Then there were the family photographs: the big one in the centre showed my mother laughing with my brother on her lap, arms twined around each other as the seven-year-old me stood alone in the shadows behind them. These artefacts were too meaningful to discard yet years of meditation had not diminished the effect they had on me so I kept them safely locked away out of sight and out of mind. I dropped the newsletter with the others and went back downstairs.

    After dinner, as always, I arranged my mat on the floor in the Sanctum, lit the candles and settled down to meditate. As my breathing slowed and grew deeper the sparkling mist gathered around my body. As I inhaled I was bathed in the soft, gentle light. I relinquished the physical and dissolved into pure consciousness. Sinking deeper I felt the familiar tingle as a soft, white down cocooned my skin. My limbs stretched, unfurling like a ship's sails and as I continued to descend they billowed, catching the pure energy of love. And I flew. My snow white wings carried me on, over sleeping houses, hospital beds, city centres.

    The sparkling mist of purity and light swirled within me. As I inhaled it took form, becoming a ball of white energy. I held it for an instant glorying in its cleansing power. Then as I exhaled I sent glowing prisms of light from the tips of my wings and I delivered my blessings.

    "To Caroline, to Louise, to Tom, and to Calum – you are powerful and loving and have nothing to fear. And to Rovena – recognise the value of your relationship. The uncertainties will evaporate and you will experience great love."

    As I returned to my earthly body, I shook out my limbs and opened my eyes, exhilarated by the powerful healing gifts I had bestowed.

BLESSINGS

In the garden next morning I drank peppermint tea from my favourite cup decorated with angels as the golden sun nourished my soul. I only had two appointments that day as Tuesday afternoon was reserved for visiting my mother at Beechwood Nursing Home. Throughout the morning my mind kept straying to Calum and Rovena. I was eager to hear what positive effects my meditations had had on her.

After a lunch of crisp raw vegetables and home-made hummus I did a thirty-minute meditation for my mother. It would ease the pain of her arthritis and open her heart to the love that surrounded her. As I drove to Beechwood House I hummed along to Enya on the CD player and smiled in satisfaction as all the traffic lights turned green before me.

As always my mother was alone in her room gazing out of the window to the woods and as always a brief twist of her lips was the only sign that she knew I had arrived.

"Isn't it a glorious afternoon!" I beamed

"It might have been till two minutes ago. What do you want?" came her response.

"I've come to see how you are because I love you, Mum. You know that."

"Love? You only turn up here every week out of a sense of duty. Makes you feel all pious. Love's got nothing to do with it. Now your brother..."

"How is George? I haven't heard from him in ages. I write but... I suppose he must be really busy with work... and the children."

She ignored me and continued on her favourite topic. "I knew from the start you'd be a disappointment and I wasn't wrong."

"Mum, my business is doing really well and I love my life and who I am. I devote my life to comforting people in need. You should be proud of me."

"Proud of you? You look down your nose at everyone. You manipulate those poor inadequates who can't fix themselves and fool them into believing your mumbo jumbo. You're a parasite and a charlatan. I'm glad you love yourself because no one else ever will."

"I'm so sorry you feel that way but I've never understood why you seem to dislike me so much, Mum. I don't think I've done anything wrong."

"That's exactly my point. You think you're so perfect and no one else on the planet can live up to your standards. You're going to end up a sad, lonely old maid with a house full of cats in place of children. For God's sake, why can't you just get blind drunk some time, get a speeding fine, fiddle your tax returns, have a one-night stand, anything to rejoin the human race. Just stop being such a Pollyanna and do something reckless or selfish!"

I closed my eyes gently for a few moments channelling some positive energy into her arthritic joints then I stood up to leave.

"I love you, Mum. I'll see you next week and I'll send you some healing in my meditations."

"Don't waste your time! Send it to yourself instead. You need it far more than me."

Her words had no power to harm me. Long ago I had learned that if I chose not to be harmed, I would not feel harm. As I drove home my shoulders ached and temples throbbed and as I stopped at a traffic light I consciously relaxed the tension in my jaw. When I arrived home I noticed the red light of the answer phone was blinking. I pressed "Play".

"Er... Hi, Joanna... this is Calum."

My shoulders eased and a wave of pleasure flooded through me.

"I just needed to call you to give you an update. It seems that whatever you sent to Rovena last night had quite a powerful effect on her."

I grinned in satisfaction.

"I found a note from her when I got home from work tonight saying that... well she's left me. She's flying to Australia with her lover... and she's, she's taken the girls..." His voice cracked slightly. "Seems they flew out this morning. It's just that... I needed to let you know... I'm just tying things up here with the house and job tonight and I'll be flying out as soon as I can. I just can't live without my little girls." He took a steadying breath and continued. "Thanks to you I realise how very lucky I am. Australia's a wonderful opportunity. Anyway it's just to thank you for... well... for everything you've done for me but, well, I might never see you again... I'm sorry... Goodbye Joanna. You really are an amazing woman."

I licked my lips to stop them quivering and my eyes felt the hot needles of budding tears. I picked up the last detox herbal teabag in the caddy and dropped it into my cup. The kettle clicked off and I poured in the boiling water allowing the aromatic steam to bathe my face. I let it infuse for a minute while I tipped some more Go-Cat into Samson's bowl. He leapt gracefully up onto the work surface beside me and sent my cup of precious tea dashing down onto the terracotta floor tiles with a loud smash. I stared at the spreading mess for a second or two before it sank in.

"Oh shit... shit, shit, shit, shit, shitty shitting shit!"

The tears had started to flow now. My breath was coming out in jerky sobs. It would take at least an hour of meditation to disperse all the hurt this day had brought. The broken faces of porcelain angels stared up at me reproachfully from the tiles.

"Oh, piss off!" I shouted, kicking the shards across the floor. I heard a click-clack as Samson fled through the cat flap. His departure was yet another betrayal. My mother was right. Nobody cared for me enough to stay around.

As I walked unsteadily to the door of the Sanctum mentally gathering up the tendrils of white light which were evaporating my inner voice chided me: "Anger and self-pity are the emotions of helplessness but you are strong and wonderful and can cope with anything life brings."

"You can piss off too!" I retorted and drawing energy from my spite I squared my shoulders and turned away from the Sanctum.

The atmosphere in the attic room was thick with years of my despondency and I absorbed the cocktail of miseries which had been held back for too long. I deliberately made my way round the relics of past sorrows, picking up every photograph, re-reading every letter and remembering. Every injustice I relived kindled the flames of bitterness in my core. I wallowed in the malevolence as I knelt on the floor and the force of the emotions surging within me was almost tangible. What I experienced was far more potent than anything I had ever achieved through years of meditation.

Calum's phone message and my mother's words screamed like an aria around me, stoking the fire. I began to breathe evenly, rejoicing in the ferocity of my emotions. I breathed in all the misery and I breathed out what little virtue remained. I inhaled malice and exhaled integrity and with every breath the seething fireball grew stronger. The power surging through me was overwhelming. As I sank deeper and deeper into hatred, I began to feel the prickling sensation across the nape of my neck spreading down across my shoulder blades. But this was not the soft down from before but more jagged and coarse. I gave a sharp gasp as thorns erupted though my skin and I tossed my head, stretching my neck to either side. I felt the barbs elongate suddenly, like flick-knives forcing my arms behind me and causing my back to arch, tilting my face towards the sky. My lips no longer felt soft and moist for in their place a hard, dry carapace grew.

I sucked in a deep, urgent breath pooling the rage, the frustration, the vengeance, harnessing their potency, and with a howl of tortured ecstasy I took to the air.

Tonight I would jettison my malignant cargo. Tonight I would deliver a lethal blessing. Tonight I would take back something for myself. And high over Asia I flew… on wings black as the plague.

LOVELY AS A TREE

David Carson

As the day drew near, Tom's restiveness increased. On one level, he wanted it all to be over. On another, he wished time would stand still. And now, with only a day left, he knew he needed to concentrate on something. He decided to tackle the cherry tree. He'd been thinking about it for some time.

He crossed the hall to the back bedroom and knocked gently on his mother's door and pushed it open. The carers had just finished, and acknowledged him as they went out.

"Good morning Mum. How are you today?" He went over to the window. His mother was in her chair, a rug tucked over her lap and behind her legs.

He bent and kissed her head, moving his hand to her forehead and holding it there. He squatted down in front of her. Her hands rested on a keyboard attached to a swivel bar. She made a slight movement with her forefinger.

"Fine." The noise was tinny, indistinct. Tom said, "Are you sure?" Her finger moved again, but there was no sound. "I'm going into the garden. Some work to do. I won't be too long."

He went out the back door, crossed the yard and stood on the grass close to the flower bed. He looked at the tree. Roots were visible at the base, and the trunk was bent, crooked. He reached up and stroked the bark. Some parts were rugose, and their tiny blisters scraped his palm. Otherwise it was smooth, unresisting. He moved his hand up and down, up and down. The tree next to it, an apple, was straggly and uneven, but it still produced fruit.

He opened the garage door and went over to the chainsaw. He carried it outside, along with the petrol canister and the oil. He unscrewed the petrol reservoir and saw that it was empty. He could never remember how to mix the right proportions for two stroke, so he went back into the garage and made a calculation on a scrap of paper, gathered up the measuring jug and went outside. He combined the two in the jug and poured the mixture into the reservoir until it was full.

The oil level was low. He knew he ought really to use a funnel when he poured it in, because it was thick, viscous and crept slowly out of the plastic bottle. Some slid down the side of the saw and pooled on the ground. It reminded him of jellyfish on the shore when they went on family holidays. His mother was forever telling him to be careful not to stand on one.

He studied the tree. It was too big to cut from the bottom. He needed to start half way up the trunk, where it was thinner, sever it there, then do the remainder. He got the ladder and laid it gently but securely against the apple tree. From there he could reach over and still hold the saw with both hands.

He laid the chainsaw on its side and set the switch. He pulled out the choke and, with one foot in the handle, he yanked the cord. The engine fired. He checked that everything was working by slowly exerting pressure on the trigger. The engine barked and whined in time to the lightening rotations of the chain.

He climbed the ladder and positioned the saw. Woodchips flew like sparklers and he was half way through the trunk. He changed the position of the saw, pressed on the trigger and the trunk peeled away and fell easily to the ground, leaving a splinter of wood at one edge. He was annoyed that he had not managed a clean break, and he cut the splinter away. Softly he brushed the exposed surface clean, and looked down. It struck him that it was strange, disconcerting even, to see the familiar in an unexpected place. Like the time he met his primary school head teacher in the supermarket. All at once she seemed small and ordinary. And there was the half trunk lying on the ground, broken and unnatural. It was heavy, like an inert body, but he managed to lift it and carry it to the end of the garden where he would shortly saw it into logs.

The lower part was easier to cut. Using the head of the saw he made two incisions either side of the bole. When he had cut nearly through, he pushed and pulled the trunk until it teetered and fell to the ground. It was a bit heavier than the other part, but he carried it to its resting place next to the upper length of tree.

The roots were deep and stubborn. Finally he got his axe from the shed and split, separated and dislodged them. He was sweating and had to leave traces of the roots in the ground.

Next he arranged the two trunks in turn on the cutting area, and

LOVELY AS A TREE

sawed through equal lengths. He stroked each log on the cut side and enjoyed its smooth friction warmth.

When he had created several barrowloads of logs, he pushed them to the garage and arranged them against the wall. He had to pass close to where the tree had stood, marked now by an irregular circle of shavings, like whitish yellow ash, already being absorbed by the grass and earth.

He looked at his watch and was surprised that the whole task had taken barely two hours. He tidied up and went back into the house, calling out, "That's me," as he entered the kitchen and filled the kettle. He went along the hall to his mother's bedroom. The rug that had been tucked over her lap was hanging unevenly, as if she had been trying to shift her legs. And the keyboard had been pushed aside. He moved behind her and put the back of his hand against her cheek. Her skin was dry and brittle, the colour of brown paper. He rubbed her cheek gently, paused, and then saw her, bending to take a cake out of the oven, the top still covered with a sheet of baking paper, stiff and curled at the edges. He bent down to fix the rug behind her feet.

"Carol will soon be here. The doctor will probably call in. You remember he has done each day for the past week. OK?"

His mother tried to move her head. He watched her, and shared the effort she was making. She made a noise. Tom bent closer to her. He thought he made out a word.

"What was that? You mean the doctor is kind? Yes, he is."

He saw a tremor in her hand, and took it between his own. He held it to his lips, then laid it gently on her lap. His eyes stung.

He went back to the kitchen, put a teabag in the pot and added the water. After a moment he poured it into his cup. He moved to the window. Looking out at the garden, he could see already that the view was different, now that it was not obscured by the tree.

He sat down at the table.

"Hello, it's me." Carol knocked on the kitchen door with her stick and entered. "There you are. I had a wander round the garden. You've been busy."

"Yes. I needed to do something." He studied Carol. She didn't seem any different – her iron grey hair was still tight to her forehead, and her intense blue eyes contrasted with her dull-coloured cardigan and brown skirt. He thought they were the same clothes she had been wearing for the past week. Up till recently he called her auntie, but lately she had become plain Carol. They were equals in all of this, he thought. She was his mother's best friend, almost like the sister she didn't have. It was natural that Carol should take on this responsibility, this role.

"How is Maureen today?"

"I'm not sure. A bit agitated, although it's difficult to know."

Carol placed her stick against the table and sat down heavily. "She was better before that stroke episode. At least you could understand her. There was communication. Amazing really, after all she had been through, all that time in hospital."

Tom shifted in his chair.

"That's just my point. Now, I'm not so sure about that."

"Tom, remember, she had made her decision. That hasn't changed."

"But I'm worried."

Carol sighed. "Of course you are. We both are. It's a big responsibility."

Tom fiddled with his cup.

"It's not just that. So far, she's been calm, resigned almost. But today, she's different."

"What do you mean?"

Tom got up and looked out of the window. "She's not using her board. She's restless, trying to move," he turned to Carol, "and to speak."

"Look, Tom, none of this is easy."

"Carol, I'm not imagining things. I'm really concerned that she's trying to tell me something."

"What?"

Tom rubbed his neck. "She said something like 'kind', but it might have been 'mind'. Maybe she's changed it."

"And maybe you're projecting your wishes on to her." Carol sighed. "We should wait for the doctor. He'll be here soon. And let's remember how clear Maureen was, how certain, after her diagnosis."

Tom nodded. He said, "Let's go into the garden and look out for the doctor."

Carol followed Tom, hobbling slowly round to the side of the house. She flicked at some leaves and stones with her stick. The day was warm.

LOVELY AS A TREE

"You're looking a bit red, Carol. Are you not too hot in that cardigan?"

"No, I'm fine. I love this garden, you know. And not just because of what's in it. When Dick and I came back from Kenya, your mother and I spent many an hour making diagrams, studying catalogues and visiting garden centres. Maureen was the expert, I was the help, but I felt I played a real part in creating and maintaining it. It was just the sort of thing I needed to be doing at that time."

She limped on round to the back of the house, stopping underneath the fir tree at the corner of the vegetable patch. Tom stood next to her.

"I dug the hole and manoeuvred the roots in to it, stamped the earth and watered it. Now look at the size of it."

"And its shadow. Covers half the growing area."

Carol made her way back to the yard. Tom went ahead and got a chair and placed it in the shade. Carol sat, sighed and relaxed her stiff leg. She closed her eyes. A slight breeze ruffled at her skirt and rustled in the grass. "A garden is good," she said quietly, "a place of cycle and repetition, growing and maturity, of time passing, and always a sense of renewal. I owe Maureen a lot."

She opened her eyes as a car turned into the yard. A young man got out, clutching a black bag..

"Good afternoon, Mrs Robertson, Tom. A fine day for being outside. At least, if the circumstances were better. How is the patient?"

Tom grimaced, and Carol answered.

"Tom thinks she's been... unsettled."

"And what did you think?"

"I haven't actually seen her today."

"Oh. Well, let's have a look."

When they entered the bedroom, Tom put a finger to his lips.

"She's sleeping."

"Probably a good thing. In fact, it would be fine if that lasted until tomorrow."

Tom cleared his throat, but it was Carol who spoke first.

"Doctor, do we really need to wait? We know what Maureen wants, even if this stroke thing has... has clouded the waters. Can't you, can't you do it now?"

"For God's sake, Carol! What are you saying? Were you not

listening?" Tom turned to Doctor Boyd. "You see, she was different this morning. I don't think we can assume that she still wants to… end it all."

Doctor Boyd shook his head. "I'm afraid that's exactly what we have to assume. All the circumstances were in order when she made her decision. You were there as next of kin, and Mrs Robertson was nominated as, and agreed to be, the supportive friend, as per the legislation. A date was proposed and confirmed, to allow for any necessary business to be transacted. That date is tomorrow. Unless the patient says otherwise. And that is not going to happen."

Tom stared at the doctor. "How well you prepare your speech."

"Well, it's true that this is not my first case. Nor will it be my last. The change in the law is proving, em, popular, if I can put it that way."

Tom turned away in disgust. "I can't accept that. There must be another way."

Carol took hold of Tom's arm. "Nothing has really changed, at least not on Maureen's part. It's you, and that is completely understandable."

Tom pulled himself angrily away from her. "Christ. It's like death row."

He pushed his way out of the bedroom, along the hall and into the yard. He kicked over the chair and stumbled on to the lawn. He knelt down next to the roots of the cherry tree and scratched at the grass, pulling out handfuls of dirt and sawdust. He rubbed them in his face and they fell, sodden, on to the earth

JEHOSEPHAT

Joyce McKinney

He is a rather shambling, untidy figure – probably because his blue security guard uniform hangs loosely on his skinny frame. He walks awkwardly as if his heavy boots are ill-fitting and hurt his feet. This does not prevent him from moving around at some speed when required and we will see him first as he reaches the gate first to unlock it to let us drive in and again when he clomps off ahead of us to the garage to open the door and start hauling out luggage or shopping.

He has a wide welcoming smile – always, and a special word for the children who skip around him as they head for the back door. They try to drag him off towards a football or the swing but if he is busy they are made to wait. Nothing is allowed to divert his attention when he is 'on the gate' and he will be off back to his post under the tree by the entrance in case the buzzer goes and he has to let someone else in.

Impossible to know what age he is. He has a very young wife and three small children – one a baby. He brought them all to visit when the youngest was born and this child has been given my name. This is a matter of some concern to me for I am unsure of the obligations such an honour has placed upon me.

He is a Luo from Kisumo on Lake Victoria. He offered to take us there to meet his family and show us the farm.

Jehosephat is a Born Again Christian and one of the first things he wanted to know when he first met us was "Had we been saved?"

Not being reassured by our hesitant answer that first time he continued to ask the same question each time we arrived on a visit.

We have been to his church for he invited us to a friend's wedding, a joyous, noisy and quite unforgettable experience. The service was lengthy and the small tin-roofed building had quickly reached a temperature that made even breathing quite a trial. Yet no-one took off a jacket or a tie and the bride in flowing taffeta and veil had a chubby florid face that positively glowed with sweat. The singing in an African church is a happy uninhibited expression of faith and when the warm-up group has been in action for half an hour the congregation is raring to go. Those who feel inclined dance in the aisles as they sing

They made us so welcome at the party, stuffing the children with sticky sweet cakes and insisting on us all joining in the dancing. Jehosephat surprised us by being a star turn at the dancing so was it only those awful boots that made him seem clumsy? He was a different man to the one we thought we knew. His slim agile body gyrated to the beat of the drums and his feet stamped and shoulders twitched and they cleared a space for him between the tables. His enthusiasm was contagious, the drum beat compulsive and he was soon joined by half the wedding party and special finery was forgotten as people gave themselves up to sheer enjoyment.

It was late when we got home, tired and dusty and the throb of the drums went on beating in our heads for most of the night.

Jehosephat's family and many of their friends lived in Kibera, the sprawling shanty town on the edge of Nairobi. If the water was cut off it happened there first. If there were fights and killings and police had to be sent in, it was likely to be Kibera. It was not safe to leave theirs huts after dark and women in labour often died from lack of medical help because they could not get out to find a doctor. There were frequent fires in the huts because cooking was done inside when it was dark or the weather was bad and the small stoves were easily over-turned in the crowded space. There were a few public showers but the queues to use them were long in the mornings and the walk to work was two miles for people like Jehosephat.

It was always a mystery to us how people emerged from such a place with clean white shirts and pressed suits to work in the town. Jehosephat's blue uniform trousers had crisp newly ironed creases every day and when the family came to visit the children were in frilly frocks with their hair tied up in ribbons. Children walking along the roads to school in the mornings were in school uniform, clean and smart, shoes polished and school bags on their backs.

When we had water at our house and the Kibera supply had been cut off Jehosephat used to fill a kerosene tin from the tap in the compound and carry it all the way home on his head.

It was reassuring to have him at his post early every morning. He got rid of unwelcome callers, scorpions behind the furniture, snakes

JEHOSEPHAT

on the veranda and scared off a menacing Sykes monkey that was sitting on the sofa ready to defy all-comers when we got back from shopping. Sykes are *big*, man-sized monkeys with nasty sharp-looking yellow teeth. As the intruder made for the window with Jehosephat brandishing a garden hoe at his behind, he snatched at the house plants he passed and stripped off flowers and leaves in a bad-tempered display of his annoyance at being made to move on.

So how did Jehosephat come to be in the city? And why was someone of such obvious attributes minding our gate and eking out a tiny salary in a miserable filthy slum?

"I have four brothers back on the farm in Kisumu," he told us. "All have wives and families. My wife, she belong Nairobi and her family is Kikuyu. She like this place over Kisumu. She get job for Mission people at Thika and one day maybe we move there and they give me job too. Too much corruption for our country and not good life for children in Nairobi. Politics bad, police bad, only thing for people like us, is go away."

It was Friday. Friday the tenth of September. The sort of day one doesn't forget. It had been very hot and the morning dawned with the promise of yet another uncomfortable day, the sky that almost viscous African blue and not a cloud to be seen. We had been hoping for some rain to relieve the clammy atmosphere and we should have had some showers by then. We did see the odd flicker of lightning around the horizon so perhaps it had rained somewhere.

Florence put water from the fridge out on the veranda. The pipe supplying the tap in the garden which everyone used was in the full sun and the water from it would be almost undrinkable by nine o'clock. After breakfast the children brought their toys through to the lounge and played on the carpet under the big fan.

"Jehosephat, he sick," Florence informed us as she passed through on her way to start cleaning the bedrooms.

I could see him down the drive by the gate when I went out to water the plants at the front of the house and soon afterwards he was at the back door mug in hand asking for water – the bucket on the veranda was empty.

"You alright , Jehosephat?" I was alarmed at his appearance, at his nasty greyish pallor and bloodshot eyes.

"I get small fever. Too much thirst." And he was off back to his post.

Joyce McKinney

From time to time I went to the window to see if things were alright but he was there by the gate as usual.

"Water for Jehosephat." Someone else was at the door with an empty mug but before he could deliver it there was a general hubbub and the sound of running feet.

"Make you come, Missus," the gardener shouted. "Jehosephat, he fall for ground."

We pulled his floppy and amazingly light body off the pathway and into the shade and I ran back to the house to phone for an ambulance. I knew he was very sick.

I thought the ambulance would never come and when it did it was a rather rusty pick-up. They heaved him into the back of the vehicle and were off while I was still leaning over the side trying to straighten him out to make him more comfortable. One blue-trousered leg with its heavy boot dangled over the tail gate but he would know nothing of that journey. He had never stirred since he had fallen.

The children were inconsolable and it was several hours before I could get any news from the hospital.

"Dat man, Jehosephat Onyango, he D.O.A. – malaria and pneumonia."

With that brief heartless message the phone clicked at the other end leaving me feeling so helpless. Was that all there was to be said of someone like Jehosephat? It had all happened too fast. Just the day before he had been up on a ladder helping to cut the overgrown creeper off the back wall and laughing and joking with the children as they soaked their clothes trying to water the garden.

I would have to get a message to his wife out at Thika and as I searched for the number of the Mission I thought about how I would break the news to her. When I got through to them someone went off to bring her to the phone and the sound of that little anxious voice made me forget everything I had meant to say.

"It's Jehosephat..." and I got no further. I heard the intake of breath and then the keening, that heartbreaking expression of grief and despair which no words of sympathy could break through.

My small son wrapped his arms around my legs as I stood there still holding the phone. I sat down then on the sofa with him on my knee and as he clung to me I buried my face in his soft hair.

Continuing Education Courses for Adults

A wide range of short day time and evening classes and Saturday workshops are available to the public at the University of Dundee including:

Art & Design	Jewellery Design
Art History	Literature
Behavioural Studies	Opera Appreciation
Botanic Garden	Personal Development
Business Skills	Philosophy
Child Development	Poetry
Counselling	Psychology
Creative Writing	Reiki
Film & Media	Science & Nature
Genealogy	Social Studies
History	Textile Design

Courses also run in Perth and Angus.

For further information and enrolments contact
Continuing Education
Tower Building
University of Dundee
Nethergate
Dundee DD1 4HN
01382 381125
conted@dundee.ac.uk
www.dundee.ac.uk/conted